A cabin full

of crime stories

Written by

Jude St Clair

Published by
Jude St Clair

© 2018 Jude St Clair

Jude.StClair@hotmail.com
www.judestclair.weebly.com
Mandurah - Western Australia
ISBN: 978-0-6481952-1-4

Acknowledgements

This book would not have been possible without some assistance (who am I kidding? *LOTS* of assistance!), support and encouragement.

I would like to acknowledge colleagues and friends who helped with reading, feedback and editing the many stories in this book, and some that didn't even make it in!

Special thanks go to a select group of Beta Readers (including Mum, Dad, Shane and Martin) who have persevered through many re-writes and still haven't given up on me!

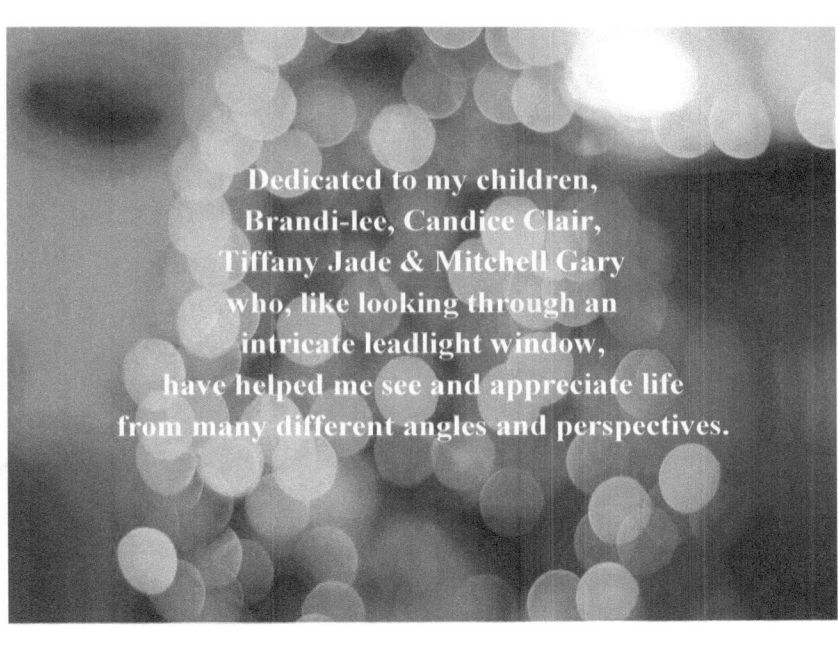

Dedicated to my children,
Brandi-lee, Candice Clair,
Tiffany Jade & Mitchell Gary
who, like looking through an
intricate leadlight window,
have helped me see and appreciate life
from many different angles and perspectives.

**Other books by
Jude St Clair**

2017 A hammock full of short stories…

Contents

On a Mission

Garry growled at the checkout girl. "Bloody highway robbery," and handed over the $56.30 the cash register had totalled for his groceries. He gathered his items, throwing them into a couple of bags moaning, "Don't even bloody pack 'em for you any more … what's this world coming to?"

Shuffling out of the local store, he headed for the parking lot. When he had been a boy, growing up in this neighbourhood, he'd seen this corner start out as a convenience store.

Since then it had been transformed into a gas station, a drive through bank, a seafood restaurant and now it was back to a convenience store again. He'd seen a lot of changes over thirty-two years, some for the better – including the campaign to stop logging and keep the remaining Russell Ridge Forest.

The local movement had demonstrated and lobbied for over five years and had finally won. Now there were 500 acres remaining of the beautiful forest he grew up in. Some changes he personally considered were for the worse – the influx of residents caused by the new mine in the late nineties, the new school which attracted young families, although

1

many of them had moved on now, since the mine had started laying folk off a couple of years ago.

The population had gone back down to near its original 2400, which Garry was quite pleased to see. He much preferred it to be nice and quiet around here, it was better for his line of 'work' - he snickered at his own joke. Garry's truck was parked at the end of the lot. It stood all by itself, alone on the gravel under a shady tree, symbolic in some respects of the driver.

He had always been a bit of a loner, even as a young boy at school. Thankfully his parents lived in a remote, secluded part of the forest, and he had been raised very much away from mainstream civilisation.

He had attended formal school in town for a few years, but then had been home-schooled by his parents. They had a little house situated at the end of an access lane for the Russell Ridge Forest water maintenance crew. Since the water from the lake was no longer pumped regularly for the mine, the access road hadn't been used now for many years.

His great grandparents had built the shack there back when homesteaders were given a little land from the government to settle and farm. The farm house had grown a little as each generation added to it, and his grandfather had purchased some extra acres from the council to add crop paddocks and room for more animals.

Garry and his twin brothers Jonas and Frederick were taught the basics at formal schooling, but most of their education came from working on the farm with their father and Uncle Ned, his twin.

Twins had run rampant in the Henderson family, with every generation, going back fifteen decades, turning out at least one set of twins.

The three boys had grown up tough. Uncle Ned and passed on when they were only children and they were forced to learn respect for the benefits of getting up with the sun, hard work, and heading off to bed early. They had chores and responsibilities their father would expect from them and punishments in the Henderson family were mainly corporal. "Spare the rod, spoil the child," his father would say as he whipped one of them three times for not completing a chore or doing something he considered 'out of line'.

Not that he was a particularly God-fearing man, but he did let their mamma go to church each Sunday with the boys. Sometimes Garry thought it was only so she could bring home a 'charity bag' – a box of groceries and other essentials that the good ladies of the church would gather during the week, make up into boxes for the needy, and dispense after church on Sundays. He would send her off with a smirk in the morning and welcome her home with "And how was God today dear?" as he unloaded the box from the car.

Garry couldn't remember his father ever going to church himself. In fact, after the axe incident he distinctly remembered his father using some language to describe God and Jesus that would have made a sailor blush, let alone the church ladies.

He secured his groceries in the back of his truck and headed off slowly through town, glancing at the boarded-up shops along Main Street, smiling as he thought of his mamma when he passed the church, scowling at the graveyard where she and his brothers now lay at rest. He didn't like to think about the accident much, but occasionally it got to him and he would shed the odd tear, get stirrings of anger or feel the emptiness in the pit of his stomach that he had first felt upon being told.

He remembered that day so clearly. It had been a Tuesday, nearly seven years ago now. The first Tuesday in December, he knew because it had been cold, and a light snow had fallen early. Garry had woken up, dressed in his old dungarees and the warm woolly jumper one of the church ladies had knitted for him last winter. He finished his daily feeding and watering of the chickens and ducks, then his other morning chores.

The axe had been blunt, so he'd spent a large amount of time trying to sharpen it as his father had taught him. He wasn't quite as strong as the older boys, Jonas and Fred, being four years older, so it naturally took him longer than he had expected to sharpen the log splitter. He had been concentrating so hard he hadn't even heard his mother call him, several times apparently, so when his father came looking for him, angry because he was holding up the breakfast, he was startled.

Old John Henderson was not known for his understanding, or his good humour, so upon finding his son taking a couple of minutes to smoke a cigarette after sharpening the axe he immediately jumped to the conclusion that the boy was trying to get out of his chores and gave him a huge clip around the ears - with his closed fist. Unfortunately, Garry had been trying to stand up right at that moment, and had lost his

4

balance and had fallen straight on to the up-turned axe. His right hand had been all but completely severed and blood was gushing everywhere. This, combined with Garry's bellowing, had just made Father even angrier.

He could see his mother's face clearly – the horror, when she had seen him being carried in by his father, blood pouring from the wound across his wrist.

The young lad remembered them all piling into the truck and his father driving to the small hospital outpost in town. He flashed back to the pain and the lovely nurse who came and sat with him and held his hand, so it didn't completely fall off.

She gave him some tablets and a needle, and the pain eventually dulled to just an awful throbbing ache. Everything was so clean here, and quiet, it was very peaceful.

The doctor had explained to Father that he would have to perform surgery to re-attach Garry's hand and that he might never get feeling back into his fingers or use the hand for normal things again. The boy knew this would make his father furious. Not being able to do his chores and pull his weight around the farm would render him useless in his father's eyes, a dead weight. The doctor insisted that Garry would have to remain in the hospital for up to a week, although he explained that because it was a work-related accident the government would pay the costs involved.

He'd hoped this would soften the blow for his father, but no, the last he saw of him was a very angry man, stomping towards the door, turning back to call his family to join him. Mother had stopped to kiss him, whispered to him that he was her angel and to be brave. The boys just smiled awkwardly and ran quickly to catch up to their father, and then they were gone.

Garry spent the rest of that day having surgery on his hand and was groggy for most of the next day, so it wasn't till Thursday that the doctor, the nice nurse and a policeman came to see him in his bed. They had sat very close and although the policeman had started the talk, it was the nurse who took over, and held Garry's good hand while she broke the news that his father had been involved in an accident on the way home from the hospital and the truck had rolled several times, ending up down the ravine that runs alongside Russell Ridge. No-one had survived the fatal crash.

Garry had difficulty comprehending it all at first, not fully understanding that everyone was gone. It was simple things that bothered him.

He remembered asking lots of questions. Like how was he going to get home? Jonas and Fred had been given driving lessons a couple of years ago, but father had never thought Garry had needed them, so he couldn't drive even though he was more than old enough. Who was feeding the animals? How much damage was there to the truck? The next day was when the reality sunk in. He had spent the day with a hollow feeling in the pit of his stomach and he threw up for hours.

He shook his head as if to rid himself of those thoughts. It was always hard around this time. Sometimes he wished he could just go to sleep in late November and wake up just before Christmas. Garry had always loved Christmas. He and his mother had a special bond over Christmas.

They both loved to decorate the house. They were only allowed to use decorations they could make themselves of course, there was no money for 'such frivolity' according to Father. They would do it while singing Christmas carols, when father was out tending to the animals or the crops or hunting rabbits and foxes with the twins.

Mother would squirrel away a few cents here and there and would buy some extra food for Christmas dinner to supplement the oversized charity box the church would give the regulars at Christmas time. She would cook a roast chicken with trimmings, pumpkin pie and biscuits with homemade gravy. For dessert she would bake an apple tart or bread and butter pudding, Garry's favourite.

After dinner, when the dishes had been done, they would sit around the fire and mamma would sing Christmas carols or ballads and they would have warm milk and homemade fruit cake.

Father would grumble a little about the expense, but generally it was the one day of the year that he seemed to enjoy, and he would usually end the evening reading from one of the old Charles Dickens or Thomas Hardy books off the shelf in the front room.

Garry found it difficult to cope with the loss of his family during the lead up to the festive season but was over the bulk of the sadness once it got to two weeks out from Christmas Day. He would buy an advent calendar but would only start it with twelve sleeps to go. He enjoyed opening the little windows each day and revelled in the little chocolate, a token luxury that his father would never have allowed.

Thinking of his mother, he'd prepare a feast for Christmas day, most of which would end up as tomorrow's meal for the chickens, the pigs or the goat, but that was ok. As long as the food was on the table on Christmas day he felt a little bit of Mother stayed with him.

He slowed down to take the turn that would lead him past the Ridge and the ravine and up to the entrance to the forest where he lived. He said a quick "I love you mamma," under his breath as he passed the spot where his father, in his furious rage, had lost control of the truck and gone over the edge, killing his kin.

As he pulled into the access road Garry thought about the farm and how much it had blossomed under his care. At first the officials assigned to Garry's case were dubious about his being able to manage to live there alone. At twenty he was legally an adult of course, but with no education and such a sheltered life, they had put his mental age at about fifteen.

The hospital got Garry to agree to having some home-help, including a nurse visit him every day for a month when he got discharged, and the doctor in charge had arranged for a social worker, Bettina, to be assigned to him. A good-natured, older, Italian woman, Bettina took the boy under her wing as it were, and over time they had bonded and become close.

She had stayed with him and talked for hours, on many occasions, letting him cry and vent his anger and never judging him. Then, as promised by the hospital, she had turned to organising some home-help for Garry, until he could learn to live with his new disability and cope with the grief of losing his family.

The home-help Bettina arranged came in the form of a nurse, Sally-Anne, who visited each day for a month. Sally-Anne assisted Garry with simple tasks he could not perform for himself like washing and keeping up with housework.

It also included two young men who were doing community service through the local penitentiary and their supervisor, who came four days a week to feed and look after the animals (unfortunately three ducks and a pig had died during those first few weeks while Garry was in hospital).

They tended the crops and vegetable garden, ploughed the fields, and did some minor repairs around the farm. It wasn't long before Garry's rehabilitation meant that he was able to assist the boys, and it had been two years now since he had required any help at all on the farm.

Garry had turned the barely self-sufficient homestead into a thriving market garden and he produced and sold vegetables; some fruit; eggs, both chicken and duck; and some of the finest apple cider in the county. He had invested the money he received from the insurance company (praise be to Mother who had taken out a little policy many years ago without telling Father) and the government wisely.

The ladies at the church had sent the assistant pastor, who had an accounting degree, around and he'd spent months advising Garry on the best way of spending his money. He had upgraded to some modern farm equipment, installed rain water tanks, taken a class in cider-making technology and added three new outbuildings over the past few years. He was proud of what he'd done and took care to ensure his produce was always of the best quality and completely organic.

Pastor Lucas also had a marketing degree, so had enjoyed being a part of the new project he undertook with Garry. Russell Ridge Farms truly blossomed under his guidance.

Apart from Bettina, the home-help nurse Sally-Anne and Pastor Lucas, Garry was a bit of a loner. The folk around town didn't like him much, probably due to his somewhat gruff attitude, which no doubt stemmed from his upbringing, but he didn't care. He was proud of his achievements and loved his little farm on the edge of the forest. He had a couple of people in his life that he trusted, what more could anyone want out of life? He didn't even regard his farm as 'work', he loved his simple, fulfilling life.

"Oh, Garry, I'm so glad you're home honey, I've had an awful time trying to get the lids on to the new jam jars we're using for the marmalades, and the baby is kicking like he's an international soccer star for goodness sake. Where are the groceries? Did you get the extra sugar I need for my cooking?" his wife chattered away as she came up to his window in the truck. She always brought a smile to his face, every time he saw her he seemed to fall in love all over again. That hadn't changed at all over the past seven years.

From the lovely, shy little nurse who held his hand the very first day at the hospital. The one who had gone on to volunteer for the position as home-help/rehab nurse when it was put up on the notice board - to this, his beautiful blushing bride, who was very pregnant with their first child. They had been married for nearly three years and he was happy that they had finally made a success of the farm, so that now they could start raising their family.

Sally-Anne was driven with regards to the business, making sure he went on long trips to distant towns, expanding their markets, increasing their range of products. She had never appeared interested in starting a family. She always had their best interests at heart, but he was happier now they had reached a point in their lives where she could see the benefits of beginning their family. He had spent a lot of time convincing her, but finally he managed to get the message through. They weren't getting any younger, they were set financially, and if they were going to have six children, as he had planned, they were best to start now.

He opened the door, hugged his loving wife and carted the groceries inside, all the while listening to her chatter about her day, adoring the fact that she doted on him, that *his* happiness made *her* happy, and that their relationship was nothing like that of his mother and father.

Opening the door to the cottage he noted that it was spotless. Sally-Anne must have spent half the morning cleaning and what was that beautiful smell coming from the kitchen? There were wonderful smells constantly permeating his house from that kitchen. Yes, he could smell the marmalade of course, but there was also the smell of a lamb roast and vegetables emanating from the front of the house. YUM! Roast was his favourite meal. As a kid he could count on one hand the times they had been able to afford a roast dinner, and now they usually had it once a week, sometimes even for lunch, like today.

He carried the grocery bags to the kitchen and spied the new batch of marmalade with the bright red topped jars they were starting to use. Sally-Anne had designed the logo herself...it displayed the words *Russell Ridge Farms* over a little apricot tree, with a small boy resting underneath eating a fresh apricot, picked off that very tree. It wasn't obvious to the naked eye, but if you looked closely, with a magnifying glass, you could just make out the scar on the little boy's wrist. It was Garry of course, and he was so proud that his beautiful wife had made this perfect label to incorporate his imperfection.

Garry scrubbed his hands and set himself straight away to the task of putting the lids on all the jam jars, twisting them tight to seal them. There were over sixty-five in total which they would offer for sale at next month's county fair. Loading them into cartons, he then moved them into the basement, where they would remain until he carted them off to the fair.

As he was about to leave, Garry spied a tiny amount of sand on the floor in the corner by the washing machine. Not sure why he even noticed it, he went over and took a closer look. There was no reason why there would be a little mound of sand there, as this basement had solid cinderblock walls and cement floors. It had been used as a laundry/storage room for many years and, as with the house above, Sally-Anne kept it immaculate.

Garry bent down and studied the area, he ran his hands along the floor and picked up a bit of the sand. It was certainly sand, it looked like the same sand as outside the window, but the window was on the other side of the room. Peering at the wall more intently, he found a small hole, about six inches up from the floor with a couple of grains of the same sand in it.

He knew the wall on this side of the room backed on to a tiny wood cellar that was only accessible from the outside of the building. In fact, it had been boarded up for ages now as they had no need to store wood. He had installed gas heating in the house years ago.

"C'mon honey, I have one more box of jars here ready to go," his wife's voice floated down the stairs.

"Sure thing, on my way," he answered, brushing the sand off his hands.

Garry brought down the last box and turned off the light, closed the door and returned to the kitchen to his wife. "How long till lunch Sal?" he enquired.

"About half an hour. Is that ok?" his wife replied.

"Sure thing. I'll just go feed the animals and clean up the tools I used earlier. Back soon." Garry passed by Sally-Anne, pausing to kiss the top of her head, and then he disappeared out the back door towards the feed shed.

After feeding the animals, putting some gardening tools away and locking the sheds, he decided to take a quick look at the wood cellar. That sand had been playing on his mind. The cellar had two big wooden doors set on an angle into the garden bed that ran along the side of the house. It was partially obscured from view by the big, bushy delphiniums his mother had planted there when they first moved in to the farm. It was the one plant that Sally-Anne had let run wild in the garden. She had told him she loved it, and it would be a beautiful reminder of his mamma, so he too had never trimmed it and had let it grow to fill that corner of the garden.

He found the doors and was surprised to notice a padlock,

not remembering ever having put a lock on them, and noticing that it was shiny, even relatively new looking. Garry went to the little gardening shed behind the house and located the box in the bottom drawer of the tool cupboard where they stored spare keys to the cider shed, the spare keys to the truck and other odd keys, some so rusted they would not even be able to be used any more.

There was a small padlock size key, all silvery and polished sitting in the bottom of the box. He was sure he'd never seen it before, but maybe his dad had installed the lock before he died. He returned to the padlock and sure enough, it unlocked it. The doors opened without a squeak, which had him amazed again. Everything in and around the farm house squeaked. It was something Sally-Anne was always on his back about.

She hated the rusty gate squeaking, the noise the hinges on the cider shed made after the rains had warped the doors a little. She was constantly reminding him to oil the garage door where she kept a little Honda for driving into town for supplies.

Garry proceeded to enter the cellar, down the steep stairs into the dark, slightly musty room below. He thought there was a light, with a pull chain to turn it on, off to the right of the door if his memory served him correctly. After waving his hands around, feeling a little foolish as he jumped with fright after encountering a giant cobweb, he finally found the chain and gave it a tug. The pale orange single bulb he was expecting to turn on was now a bright, LED light and illuminated the room like a spotlight.

Garry absorbed the sight with amazement. The cellar had been transformed into some sort of hospital-grade theatre. It had all the equipment you would expect to find in a surgery and was pristine clean. He heard a moaning noise, that brought him out of his daze. Looking to the far right of the room he saw, shackled to a chain set in the wall, a girl. Maybe in her twenties. Long brown hair, slim build, half covered with a blue blanket. She was in some sort of hospital gown, scrubbed clean and seemed to be drunk or drugged or something. She was moaning in her sleep. Garry was stunned. Frozen to the spot. He just had no idea what was going on here, right under his home. "Oh honey. I'm sooo sorry," Sally-Anne's voice startled him, and he turned and stumbled slightly. He put his hand out to steady himself, straight into that damn cobweb again.

"Arrgghh," he exclaimed and danced around trying to wipe the cobweb from his injured wrist, "Good Lord Sal, you scared the life out of me!"

"Sorry about that. I was worried when you didn't come back from the feed shed for dinner and came looking for you," she replied, sadness creeping into her voice.

It was then that Garry registered that she was holding a gun on him. "Sal, what are you doing? What's that? Why do you have that? What is going on?" Garry was running his words into each other, so stunned with what he was seeing that he was barely coherent.

"I am really sorry, honey. Sorry you had to discover my secret lab. Sorry you had to go snooping around. I mean, it's been here for nearly three years now," Sally-Ann explained.

"I thought I was going to be able to continue my work here without ever being discovered." His wife moved into the room and perched on the stool next to the surgical trolley. She motioned for him to sit on the chair against the wall, opposite the girl on the bed.

"You see, I've been carrying on my nursing work. You know when I first got the job taking care of you, working with you as your rehab nurse, I knew this was my calling. This was what I was supposed to do. Help people with their rehabilitation. However, you were quite forceful about my giving up the job when we got married, and I understood, you wanted me to help with the farm, the new cider and jam industries we were commencing. But I got bored. I found that while you were out tending animals, ploughing fields and especially when you were away, selling our wares, I would get lonely and not know what to do with myself," Sally-Anne went on, a little out of breath now as she had got herself down those stairs on her own, no mean feat for someone who is imminently about to have a baby.

"So, one day, while I was in town I met a girl. Actually, she sort of tried to rob me. She went to snatch my purse when I got out of my car, and I shoved her, and she hit her head on a parking sign. So, long story short, I put her in my car and brought her home. I locked her in the basement and spent two days talking to her and trying to teach her the error of her ways. She was sick of using drugs, she said, she needed help though, as she wasn't able to kick the habit on her own."

Garry was slumped on the chair, not believing what he was hearing.

"I kept her sedated, in the basement, and every day I helped her get through detox and eventually she was able to eat, drink and function properly, so I released her back into society three weeks later. I drove her over to Charleston and let her go at a women's shelter, while you were away on one of your trips."

"How could I not have known? Not have heard her? I don't understand how this could have gone on, under my nose." Garry was shaking his head in disbelief.

"Well honey, you are very focussed on the farm. You were so busy taking the cider classes and supervising the installation of the new buildings. You go off on your selling trips for ten days a month, to the surrounding towns, marketing our jams I never encroached on 'our' time, I only ever used my 'spare' time to help these wayward girls."

"Girls? How many girls have there been?" Garry asked, confused by what he was hearing.

"About eleven. Not counting the two that passed away," his wife replied.

"Passed away? You mean girls died here? In our house? Where are they now? What happened?" A tinge of anger was now appearing in his voice.

"Yes, sadly not everyone survives the detox process. But a twenty percent failure rate is remarkable, honey. You should be proud. Over time I have increased the facility to what you see today, and I'm proud to say that it is one of the best facilities across the state. It has the most modern, up-to-date equipment I could afford. I have studied drug rehabilitation online in my spare time and, even if I do say so myself, I am

17

very good at it." Sally-Anne looked around her make-shift hospital ward/prison cell proudly.

Her eyes had changed though, Garry thought, there was a manic, glazed look to them.

"But if you truly wanted to do good, to work again in rehabilitation, why didn't you say so? Why didn't you tell me? Why do this so secretly?"

"Well, the main reason was that after reading all the information and taking courses, I began to believe that the best possible chance for these girls was to take the severe, hard-line approach. I wasn't sure you would be totally on board with that decision, or my going back to work for that matter, especially while I was pregnant." Sally-Anne reached for a bottle of water from the box near the bench. "I concluded that the best way to commence would be with a complete detox. This is difficult and if it is done properly, as a total abstinence program, you know, when they talk about going 'cold turkey'? Well that's what I have been doing. A complete detox, with no substitute drugs to mask the symptoms, it can be brutal. I didn't want to put you through the stress of coping with that. You do so much for us around the farm," she sipped at the water and continued, "The detox then needs to be combined with intensive cognitive-behavioural therapy. Most of these girls would either not sign up for this treatment on their own, or pull out when the going got tough. So, I figured I would run a facility that would make the decision for them, that they would remain on the program until it was successful, no matter what. I would free them from their own bad decision-making and retain them here, until they were completely drug free. They would be rehabilitated, and not only could they participate in our society, but they could finally contribute to it, as a valuable member. Do you see honey? I was being like a guardian angel to them."

Garry shook his head from side to side. Slowly he began to comprehend what had been going on here, under his very roof, his house, under his own nose, literally. He looked at Sally-Anne, hardly able to distinguish his own loving, thoughtful wife from the mission-oriented, delusional woman that sat before him in this hellish place.

He stood up and made to head over to the young girl, still moaning, tossing and turning sporadically on the bed.

"Where are you going? Honey? What are you doing?" Sally-Anne stood up, the gun still in her hand.

"I'm going to check on this poor lass. I'm going to get her some help and you too my love. This cannot continue. You must know that. It is wrong. You cannot keep people against their will. Surely you can see …"

Bang!

The shot resounded off the cellar walls, deafening both of them. "No! Don't take another step," his wife instructed, as she lowered the weapon. She had fired the warning shot straight up, into the roof. It had shaken loose some sand which sprayed all over the girl, the bed and the wall behind her, the wall that backed on to the basement.

Garry realised then that the roof sand was the same as the sand he had seen in front of the tiny hole in the basement wall. The girl had obviously dug it out of the crack between the cinderblocks. She must have used a nail or something as it was tiny, just enough for a little of the loose sand from the ceiling to worm its way through.

Garry turned to his wife. "Sweetheart. I am not going to stand by and let you keep this girl here. In our cellar, against her will. She needs proper medical treatment, and you too. It's wrong. Don't you see that?" he turned away and strode over to the girl.

Bang! Bang!

Garry's face contorted as he clutched at his stomach and fell to his knees. "Sal …" that's all he managed before he fell, face forward onto the sparkling white tile floor, and his blood pooled underneath him.

"I'm sorry honey. Truly, deeply sorry. But my work here is more important than either of us individually. I must be able to continue," she put the gun aside, tucked the blanket around the girl on the bed and shushed her back to sleep.

Sally-Anne took a swig of her water and busied herself getting her husband's body on the wooden pallet she had rigged up with a pully system to get heavy items and bodies up and down from the cellar.

Two years ago, she'd organised the two boys from the village who had helped Garry with the farm buildings, to put in a second set of doors to the cellar that led from the enclosed verandah. She'd purchased a floor rug to cover them, so no-one would ever know the doors were there.

It took her a half hour to get him up to ground level and on to the dolly she used to ferry items to and from her little Honda.

20

Garry had never even noticed the dolly she had stored folded next to the little tool cupboard in the garage, he hardly ever went in there. She dragged it out to behind the cider shed where she had planted a small flower garden with a lavender hedge behind it, the year before last.

She had explained to Garry back then that she wanted this to be her own personal little garden, that she would grow flowers for the house and possibly lavender for potpourri, and that she alone would tend this garden. He had been more than happy to leave her to it, he had so much to do with tending the vegetables and crops and animals on the farm.

She spent the next hour bringing out the little digger she had convinced Garry to buy last year and using it to dig a trench, next to the other ones she had lined up behind the lavender hedge. This would make nine trenches now. She was a little ashamed at telling Garry only two of her patients had died.

The actual number was seven, and of course that horrible, ungrateful little cow that had very nearly escaped and put her whole project in jeopardy. She would be placing Garry there, right next to her. She did feel sad that Garry would no longer be around. Mostly because he provided so well for her.

He had managed to finance her under-ground operations, had looked after the farm, kept her clothed, fed and healthy. She would probably have to seek a new husband soon. There was no way she would be able to keep up her good work and take care of a damn baby. That was the only thing about Garry that really annoyed her, he had wanted a bloody family. He just couldn't leave it alone, he had talked about it continually and in the end, she'd agreed just to keep him off her back. Ultimately though, as long as her work continued, the baby, Garry, everything else was just incidental. She was a woman on a mission – God understood that, she was sure.

The Artful Roger

Sitting by a slightly open window in the office with the cool breeze wafting in, was a welcome relief after the warm day. I was finishing the Sudoku from today's newspaper and looked up when I heard it. The distinctive tap, tap, tap followed by a slight scraping sound. I got up from my desk and walked to the window ledge. I could make out the outline of a bird against the thick blackness of the night. One of the reasons I bought this property was its location on the outskirts of town. The nights out here were completely dark. No glow from suburbia. Certainly no traffic lights or street lights, and hardly ever did we get a passing car. I opened the window a little further.

"There you are my baby girl," I said softly to my raven as she tip-toed up my hand and on to my arm, "You are back safe I'm glad to see. Did you bring me my key?"

The bird understood what I wanted and opened her mouth, dropping a small key with a little red disk onto my palm. "Thank you, Penelope. What a good bird you are." I reached over to the top drawer and drew out the box of treats, giving her one, then placing them back in the drawer. She delicately took the treat and flew back to her perch in an open cage against the far wall.

I carried the key to the kitchen, rinsing it and patting it dry with paper towel, then returning to my desk and the plans I had been studying. An hour later, as I was finishing up the last of the instructions I had written out for Kirsten, I saw headlights coming down the country lane past the property and then turn into the long, winding driveway. I put the plans away and turned off the office light, saying goodnight to Penelope and checking her water bowl before I left.

"Hey honey, I'm home," Kirsten's sing song voice wafted up the stairs as I made my way down to her at the front door. "Did you miss me?"

"I certainly did my love." I admired my sultry fiancée, dressed in a slinky, hip-hugging red velvet cocktail dress, with high, strappy red stilettos, her bleach-blonde hair looking wild and untamed. I guessed she had driven with the roof down on her convertible all the way home. "How was the ballet? How is your sister?" I asked her, leading her by the hand to the kitchen, where I would make her a hot chocolate before bed. I knew she adored the ballet.

"Oh, she's good. Still got ups and downs with that lazy husband of hers, but it looks like he's finally got a job. A carpentry assistant or something. Anyway, hopefully he will be contributing now, instead of living off Amy continually. Surprisingly, the ballet was good. They did Swan Lake justice for once. I don't know why they do it every blooming Christmas. Why don't they pick something else for a change? They have a new choreographer and they most certainly have a new costume lady. Amy was saying that someone made a large donation in August that they specifically earmarked for the Christmas production, so they were able to get some nice new costumes. Thanks babe for the cuppa." Kirsten lowered her head and sipped at her mug of hot chocolate, not noticing my wry smile. "I'm going to get changed then you can fill me in on your night." She bent to give me a peck on the cheek and disappeared upstairs.

I did my nightly rounds of the house, double checking the alarm, the doors and windows and the gun cabinet. I closed the blinds in the laundry then headed upstairs to join Kirsten in the bedroom. I had already checked the office and locked that up for the night, so a glance into the spare room and bathroom was all that was needed up here.

"So, what did you get up to today Roger?" Kirsten asked as she slipped on her frilly negligee, then hopped into bed.

"I studied the plans for tomorrow's heist. Our Italian client has been most helpful, and I've made detailed instructions for you to read over before you leave. I think everything is organised."

"Right, so I drive over there in the morning. I guess I'll have to leave about six o'clock," Kirsten replied, then picked up her mug from beside the bed.

"I have you leaving here at 6.30, that should be plenty of time. It's no good getting there early hon, it doesn't open till 9 o'clock," I answered, as I got ready for bed. "When you get there, you will need to show ID to the teller, but go to the old dear who works at the end, I've been there several times. She can barely see without her glasses and she's too proud to wear them all the time, so chances are she won't even pick them up and put them on. The ID's pretty good anyway, it will pass her scrutiny."

Donning my Captain America pyjama's, I got into bed next to my girl and turned to face her. "I love you. I hope you know that. You are gorgeous. What on earth did I do right that I deserve to be this happy!" I snuggled in and put my head on her lap as she sipped her drink. I took a deep breath, thankful for such a wonderful woman in my life.

"So, back to the job," I said, returning to business. "The old dear will signal the guard at the door and he will come over to collect you. He will escort you to the door in the rear wall, where he will radio for it to be opened. Another guard will meet you at the door. That will be either Greg or Johnny. Both are about twenty something and dumb as donkeys. Bat your eyes, stick out your chest and all they will remember about you is your boobs. They will take you as far as the reception desk, in front of the vault and safety deposit boxes. Now the desk will be manned by Rosalie. She's only a receptionist and not very bright. Keep your boobs out as she will be impressed even more than either of the boys! Rosie, as they call her, is a very butch, slightly overweight, very desperate young lady. She's a lesbian, only twenty-three and 5' 4", with a solid build. According to water cooler talk at the bank she's only had two relationships in her life, both ended badly, so she will appreciate your … assets." I gave a laugh, and Kirsten put down her empty mug and did a little wiggle.

"Oh, you're not going to get jealous now are you my Roger Dodger?" she teased, using her pet name for me.

I made a grab for her boobs with one hand and pulled her close to me with the other. "No way, it kind of turns me on knowing you are going to use these puppies to get us over $10 million in rare coins!"

We playfully wrestled for a bit and kissed passionately.

"Anyway," I broke away and continued telling her the plan, "From there you will have to show the ID again and let her know which box number you need and sign in. You know the box number. 347. Remember? That shouldn't be difficult if you wiggle that butt of yours and distract her with these boobies!" I gave them a squeeze and she laughed. A beautiful sound and another of the many reasons this woman had me wrapped around her little finger.

"Make sure you sign the fake name from the ID. You need to be consistent. Also, she may just look at it to see what your name is if she's attracted to you."

I rolled back on to my side of the bed. "She will take you into the room and you will tell her you need to open box 347, the one we organised last month for ourselves. She will use her key and you will use yours – the one I gave you the other day that was on a blue tag. Then, go to the little desk and stare at her. She will get the message you need to be alone and will leave. There are no cameras in that room, it's a privacy thing. As soon as she leaves you can then get out the other two keys, the ones required for the client's box, the real one we want to open. The key I gave you last week is on a pinkish tag, remember. Our client gave it to me a couple of weeks ago. And this one, which is a spare copy of Rosie's key." I passed her the little key on the red tag that Penelope had brought me when she returned from her mission tonight.

I had painstakingly kept the bank manager under surveillance for over two months now. I knew where he kept the spare safety deposit box key, on a hook in the locked basement of his house. He kept a whole board of keys there, all the spares for the bank. It had a shiny red tag, so he wouldn't forget which one it was, as Rosie was notorious for leaving hers at home and Arnold, the bank manager, had been forced to send a teller or a clerk to his home several times to fetch the spare key for the day. His wife Gertie would retrieve the key from the basement for them and they would dutifully bring it back to the bank. Having the key on the shiny red tag had made it easy for her, but also particularly easy for me to train Penelope.

I had made a little frame with a window in it. First, I had trained her to open the window and fly through on my command. I always left it slightly ajar and she would use her body weight to prise it open far enough for her to ease through.

Then I trained her to pick up keys on red tags that were hidden on the other side of the window. I hung them in trees around my property and every time she'd brought them back I gave her a treat. Just like Pavlov's dog. She had always been a quick learner and had helped on many a job over the years.

From there I had expanded her training, she learned how to push the window closed then I began taking her to the park opposite the bank manager's house. The next step had involved hiding some keys on the outside of his house during the night and for the past two weeks Penelope had flown to his home every night and retrieved a key from outside the basement window.

Yesterday morning my friend Brett had gone to Arnold's home for a prearranged appointment to assess the basement for installation of a new gas meter. I had sent Arnold and Gertie a 'special offer' of half price gas for a year if they changed their provider and as expected they had jumped at the chance of an appointment to discuss it. While he was there Brett had worked on formulating a good rapport with Gertie, it's amazing what a little flattery can do to a fifty-year-old woman! He had her eating out of his hand, just like Penelope, within half an hour. Brett had her off making him a cup of tea while he inspected the basement which she had unlocked for him.

He'd said he could have taken the key right then, but that's not how we work. It would have left too much to chance. Arnold could have come home that evening and discovered it missing, he could have needed the key during the day, there were lots of unknown possibilities. I pride myself on being thorough. All he needed to do was unlock the tiny basement window and leave it ajar. There was much less chance of that being noticed as the window was high up, in the back corner behind some shelving.

Now, tonight, I had taken Penelope to the park, given the command and she had flown to the basement window, opened it and disappeared inside. I had driven home and left her to do her job. She had returned an hour later with the key, just as I had planned. If the key was discovered missing tonight it would be presumed misplaced by the careless manager, as the basement door would still be locked and there was no evidence of a break in. Penelope would have pushed the window back in with her beak as she had been trained to do so no-one would know she had been there, and it would be obvious that no person, adult or even a child, could have got through that small space anyway.

"After Rosie leaves, take the two keys and open box 5429, the client's box. Inside you will find a velvet pouch. You need to take that pouch out, empty the coins into the zippered pocket in the handbag I gave you and return the pouch to the box. Replace it and leave." Kirsten was listening intently. She was a good listener and knew not to ask questions until we had covered the whole scenario.

"The zippered pocket is lined with a new material, infused with a safe adaptation of asbestos. It has amazing heat, fire and electricity retardant properties. As you leave the bank and pass through the body scanner your handbag will go through the x-ray machine. The guards won't see the coins in the pocket, the asbestos-infused material will act as a barrier and they won't show up on the monitor." Kirsten rolled over on her side to face me. "Are you clear on the arrangements after leaving the bank?" I quizzed her.

"Yes. Straight up Main Street, turn right on to Westminster Ave and down the alley next to the butcher. The car will be parked in the lot behind the bakery. Drive to Jonestown and meet Amy for lunch at noon at the Travelodge. Home by 4pm."

I kissed my girl on the top of her head. "That's it K. Perfect. Then it's off to Rome on Friday where we relax for a couple of nights, then we meet with the buyer in Florence on Tuesday," I turned off the bedside lamp, "How about we linger in Tuscany for a week before we head home? Would you like that?"

She nuzzled in to my chest. "Mmmmm, yes, that sounds good babe. I've set the alarm, I guess we should get to sleep. We have a big day tomorrow."

The next morning dawned and by the time I awoke Kirsten had already left. I called her at 8.45am, before the bank was due to open and wished her luck. She was getting a coffee in the café next door and was all set for her part in the proceedings. She told me she would call when she got to Jonestown.

There was nothing more I could do now, so I spent the morning tidying up and looking on the internet for a nice hotel in Tuscany. The day seemed to fly past, so when the phone rang I didn't expect it to be K.

"Hey babe. All good. Picked up the package and I'm heading off to lunch. I'll see you tonight. Love you."

"Excellent. No trouble then? Enjoy your lunch. Can't wait to see you! And the package!"

"No, no problems at all. Better than expected actually. See you about four o'clock," Kirsten replied, then she was gone.

I went into the office and gave Penelope a treat. "There you go my baby girl. It all went according to plan and once again you were a big part of that!" I petted the raven and put her back on her stand.

After Kirsten got home we celebrated with a few beverages and a homecooked meal. The next few days passed slowly as we stayed close to home and laid low, preparing our bags for the continent. Kirsten called Amy who agreed to take care of the house and feed Penelope while we were gone. We had installed a hidden skylight in the attic roof where she could come and go as she pleased. It had bars on it that only a bird could fit through, so that the house remained secure.

Friday finally arrived, and we were prepared for our trip. We caught a taxi to the airport and boarded a long flight across the sea. Our booking at the Hilton in Paris meant that we were able to indulge in two days of luxury to unwind before we completed the job. Monday, we set off for Florence on the train. I had reserved us a 1st class cabin on the 9am from Paris, the longer journey, so we could catch up on some 'alone time'. We both enjoyed the train trip and its leisurely crawl through the mountains. We'd been meeting our clients in Florence or Rome once or twice a year for the past six years so had learned to fully appreciate the beautiful countryside in France and Italy.

It didn't take long on Monday to check in, and we spent the rest of the day walking the piazza's and dining in outdoor cafés. Tuesday morning, we gathered the coins and set off to meet our client in the small public waiting room at the local train station just out of the city.

He was due to meet us at noon and we made sure we arrived by then. I told Kirsten to sit in the waiting room while I bought us coffees and was just about to go out on to the concourse to do that when the Italian Polizia burst in from the station and the two other entrances, the door from outside and the janitor's room.

"Freeze!" "Hands up!" "Don't move!" People were shouting at us from every angle. I stood, hands in the air, totally gobsmacked. I glanced at Kirsten and she shrugged, not knowing what was going on and looking very distressed.

Four hours later, in the little interrogation room in the stazione di polizia, Kirsten and I had been questioned relentlessly and neither of us had spoken a word. The officials had resigned themselves that they would not be getting any information out of us and had decided to remand us in a local prigione, a prison close by, until Interpol decided how they would proceed.

"Prenderemo il prigioniero ora, grazie." The tall poliziotto signed the forms and put handcuffs on both of us. We were marched out to the security van and thrown roughly in the back, the door slammed behind us. It was a bumpy ride for the next twenty minutes, and then the van pulled over. The door opened, and we were pulled out, uncuffed, given a fresh set of clothes and shuffled into the back of a black SUV.

Kirsten and I spent no time getting changed, throwing our prison garb out the window and within a quarter of an hour we had made it to the private airfield. As we were sipping cocktails and winging our way back home, Max, one of the fake 'security guards' from the van, made his way back to the cabin and asked just how we had managed it.

"Well," I had explained to him, "I discovered that they knew about us nearly a month before the heist. It turns out that the woman I had called the 'somewhat stupid receptionist' Rosie, was in fact an undercover police officer. Interpol had been using her to keep an eye on us since the last heist, when they realised that they didn't have enough evidence to arrest us. Rosie had been planted there as soon as they had learned which bank we were going to hit. Apparently, they had bugged our phones for months, I had only discovered this about four weeks ago and had been very careful about who I told. It was funny really because Rosie later informed us that she hadn't recognised Kirsten in the blonde wig and stilettos."

I went on to explain that she is normally in sandals and has a short, dark brown bob with a fringe. It wasn't until she bent over and wiggled her boobs in front of Rosie that the undercover cop recognised the tiny tattoo of a blue rose, wrapped in barbed wire on her chest. She knew then that this imposter was Kirsten. She remembered seeing that same tattoo on my right arm in a photo taken by the Italian Polizia two years ago.

I told him that from there the operation had gone into full swing with agents following Kirsten to Jonestown, keeping surveillance on the house and then following us to Paris and Florence. They had realised we were on our way to meet the client, so it was just a matter of staking out the railway station and waiting for us. They had picked up our client about ten minutes before we arrived, and he had filled in the blanks for them. They pretty much knew everything.

Or so they thought.

In fact, upon discovering that we had been under surveillance I had decided to go ahead with the plan as it was, but we would include a twist that no-one other than Brett and our client knew about. We had purchased burner phones and had organised to go ahead with the original strategy right up to the capture…in fact, the capture and arrest were integral to the second part of the plan.

It was obvious that they would transfer us to the local prison, so it was easy enough to substitute our own security van for the real prison van. Brett's off-sider Martin had arranged to substitute a 'fake' client, an out of work Italian actor who had been duped into thinking this was all an elaborate plot for a new movie. He would be arrested, but was sure to be released once the facts came to light and naturally he was paid handsomely for his inconvenience. The real client had posed as an antique coin expert for the polizia for the past month. When he was called in to verify and authenticate the coins from this heist he had made a substitution of fake ones for the real coins and had walked straight out of the stazione di polizia with $10 million worth of coins in his asbestos material lined pocket.

"Ha, so they out smarted themselves so to speak." Max had found that amusing.

"Yes, it was the old 'artful dodger' trick from Oliver Twist. While they were busy watching what was happening to the right of them we picked their left-hand pocket!" I replied, laughing. Max sauntered off, still snickering, as I leaned over and gently kissed my beloved Kirsten's hand. I lay back in my recliner, aboard the luxury jet flying us to our new home and contemplated the exciting things that might be in store for us in New Zealand, the land of the Kiwi.

Taking Pictures with my Heart

Sue-Ellen was just finishing up for the night. This would be the last one of the final set. A beautiful old tune. *Taking Pictures with my Heart*. She doesn't remember where she first heard it, but it was most assuredly a favourite and she had been singing it for years. As the melody wafted through the room and she finished the last verse, Marcie gave her a smile and a nod from behind the bar, as she disappeared down stairs to switch off the kegs, run some water through the beer lines and close off the taps.

Jeff had already called last drinks some time ago, so there were only a few stragglers making their way to the doors. Sue-Ellen finished up, turned slowly and began to pack away her equipment.

She shut down the power to her guitar and amplifier and folded up her song book. A light tap on her shoulder startled her and she let out an involuntary squeal, jumping and losing her balance as she kicked her stool.

"S-s-s-sorry Miss, I didn't mean to s-s-s-startle you," the young man stuttered apologetically. He held his cap in his hands and was wearing the typical garb for patrons from around these parts - lumberjack shirt, thick pea coat, work boots and denim pants. He looked clean and bright-eyed and immediately Sue-Ellen smiled, and her face softened as she reassured him.

"That's fine hon, not your fault, I've just been jumpy all night. Something about those girls going missing lately has me all on edge I reckon."

"My name is Lionel, Miss. And, well, I just wanted to s-s-s-say that you have a lovely voice and thanks s-s-s-so much for singing that beautiful song. My mamma used to sing it when I was a boy. Good evening to you Miss." The young man began to turn away.

"Thank you," Sue-Ellen said and brushed his arm tenderly. "I love that song too. Thank you for coming tonight and you have a lovely evening." The young musician turned back to her bag and put the last things away as the lad smiled, doffed his cap, and went off to the side exit. She had a fleeting thought that perhaps her mother used to sing it to her too. She'd not known her real parents very long because her family had been killed in a car accident when she was four years old. She'd been adopted by a lovely couple, but they had been much older and had passed away a few years ago in the local nursing home.

"Night Sue-Ellen."

"Night hon."

The bar staff called their farewells as she made her way out the side door towards the carpark.

"G'night Marcie. G'night Jeff," she replied.

She felt proud of herself tonight. She had tackled those two new songs with gusto and they'd gone over well with the patrons. She was happy, overall, with her evening's performance.

"You earned your money tonight girl," she mumbled to herself. Noting that the light in the car park was out again, she hurried across the gravel to her beat-up Ford Focus and opened the hatchback to stow her music bag and the guitar case. From out of nowhere a hand clamped over her mouth and another pinned her right arm, forcing her to drop the guitar case on the gravel. She could taste the cotton wool on her tongue and it made her gag.

She tried to turn around to face her attacker, and she glimpsed a tiny bit of checked shirt under a dark coat sleeve before she slumped unconscious to the ground.

Sue-Ellen woke with a massive headache. Several parts of her were hurting now. Her arms were sore, her eyes hard to open. Her tongue felt swollen and the right side of her face stung. Her right leg hurt. It felt like it had gravel rash. She struggled to wiggle into an upright position but banged her head on something solid, so she lay back down again, slowly. It was very dark, and she could barely make out what looked like a wooden roof, very close to her head, a bit like the old upper bunk on her bed when she was a kid.

Her dad had custom-made the beds for her and her sister and constructed them a lot lower than normal…just like her to think of her dad right now…she couldn't help the corners of her mouth twisting into the tiniest of smiles.

Taking stock of her surrounds again, she could feel some sort of binding around her wrists and ankles - not harsh, but tight all the same. *Good grief,* she thought, *what the hell happened? Where on earth am I?* She slipped slowly back into unconsciousness.

A pounding started in her head again. Sue-Ellen realised that some time must have passed. She had been moved from that first place where she had woken up earlier. Now she could feel softness below her. Was she lying on some type of blanket? A quilt or comforter perhaps? Strangely, she also had the sense that she was moving. Perhaps on a train? In a ship's cabin? It was still dark, dark enough to see only shapes, not distinct outlines, and she was having trouble opening her eyes fully. One was very swollen.

"Hello," she tentatively tried whispering. Her voice came out like a frog's croak. "Where am I? Is anyone there?" Just uttering those words had caused the pounding in her head to resume with renewed vigour. She gave in once again to the thick fog of unconsciousness.

Later, when Sue-Ellen opened her eyes, she realised that it was daylight. Light was filtering in from a tiny round window, high up in the far wall. Her pounding head had eased to a dull ache, and she realised her wounds had been dressed. She had gauze on her leg, the side of her face and her arm. There was a small bandage near her knee. She was wearing some sort of hospital gown, although this was certainly not a hospital. It was obvious, from her first glance around, that she was lying in a bed, on some sort of boat. There were two bunks on each side of the cabin and a tall cupboard at the end of the bed. At the foot of the bed was a little shelf that held two bottles of water. The door in the far wall was closed but the door next to her head was open. She sat up slowly, taking in her surroundings, trying to think back to what had happened. All she could remember was going out to the car after the show and then falling to the ground. She shook her head groggily, muttering to herself.

After swinging her legs over the edge of the bed she attempted to stand up, stumbling as her weight seemed too much for her shaky knees to bare. Grabbing hold of the side of the bunk, Sue-Ellen began to inch forward, just a step, towards the open door. She could see now that it led to a little bathroom and slowly she worked her way along the side of the bed until she reached the doorway.

She managed to get through the opening and was turning to close the door when a voice startled her, and she banged her wrist on the door handle.

"Oh, you're awake. Are you ok?" The female voice, hesitant and shaky, seemed to float down from above.

Sue-Ellen looked up and realised the voice was coming from the top bunk on the other side of the cabin.

"Who are you? Where am I? What did you do to me? Why am I here?" she couldn't help blurting out all her questions, one on top of the other.

"Shhh," came the reply, "speak quietly or they will come back."

Sue-Ellen, feeling slightly stronger now, came back into the room and tentatively made her way towards the other set of bunks, on the far wall.

"Who? Who will come back?" she asked.

"Them. I think the oldest one is Tank, the shorter one they

call 'Stumpy' and the other one, the one in charge, he is just called 'Boss'. I haven't seen them today, so they are due to come down with some food shortly. You'd best be laying back on the bunk, pretending to be asleep, if you know what's good for you. They generally leave you alone if you do that."

The girl was raised on one elbow, looking over the edge of the bunk now. "My name is Felicity. What's yours?"

"Sue-Ellen," she managed to squeak out softly.

"I guess I was taken a few nights before you. The other girl, who came the night after me, sadly passed away yesterday. They removed her last night. They probably dumped her body over the side."

Felicity continued, "You've been here for four days now, but mostly you've been out of it. Drugged. They did that to me too, but I came out of it a lot quicker than you."

Sue-Ellen sat back down on her bunk. Four days. She couldn't remember a thing.

"There's some stuff in the bathroom to clean up with if you want. I would try and make it quick, as they hear the water running sometimes and come in while I'm naked."

Felicity's voice wavered. "I guess I should tell you that they … they … you know. While you were out cold. They did it to me too," Felicity sounded sad, "I'm sorry."

Sue-Ellen inhaled deeply. Her mind was racing. She just couldn't understand all this. She got up and went back to the tiny bathroom. Sitting on the toilet she was suddenly overcome with emotion and the tears started flooding out. She sobbed, holding her head in her hands and eventually stood up, washed her face, hands and neck with a clean face washer, while looking at herself in the little mirror above the basin. She could barely recognise herself. Her hair was a matted mess, her face black and blue with bruising. She had cuts and scratches and a gauze bandage stuck to the side of her face. "Good God woman, you look like you've gone three rounds with Mike Tyson!" Sue-Ellen managed a wry smile as she spoke to the reflection in the mirror.

"Come on, get yourself together now. You can do this." After finishing her pep talk she dabbed her face and neck with the hand towel and returned to the cabin.

"Quick, get back on to your bed," Felicity whispered urgently, "someone's coming."

Sue-Ellen barely made it back on to her bunk and threw the cover over the bottom half of her body, closing her eyes just before someone entered the room.

"How's my little blondie today?" a gruff voice asked. "Feeling better sweetie pie? I've got some lovely lunch for you. A piece of last night's lamb, some vegetables and gravy. Just like your mamma used to make," he chuckled, "and how's your friend? Back in the land of the living now I hope. We don't want any more unfortunate incidents like yesterday, do we?"

"I'm awake thank you," Sue-Ellen couldn't help but answer the man. After all, he didn't sound too bad. Maybe this was all some sort of big mistake. "Can you please tell me where I am, and what this is all about? What happened to me?"

The old man dressed in scruffy jeans and a striped sailor's shirt was almost comically cliché, with his gold earring and long beard. He put the food down on the shelf at the end of the bed and turned to her. "Ahh, we are awake then. How you feeling 'Red'? You've been sleeping for days now, you should be nice and rested."

"I feel dreadful, thank you for asking," she answered indignantly, "Will you please answer my questions. Where am I? What is happening here?"

"Don't you worry about that young lady. All you need to do is keep your mouth closed…unless the Boss asks you to open it of course," he chuckled lewdly. "Now you'll have to share that food, and don't forget to clean yourselves up. Stumpy and the Boss will be down later, and they'll be needing some company, nudge nudge, wink wink."

The old man left then and after the door closed she heard the bolt slide. "What did he mean – Stumpy and the Boss will want some company?" she asked Felicity, although she was pretty sure she already knew the answer to that. She got down from the bunk and went to inspect the food, realising that she was ravenous. She grabbed a water bottle and guzzled nearly half. "Do you want some of this food?" she asked her new friend on the top bunk.

"No honey, you go ahead. You must be starving. I'll just have my bottle of water please."

Sue-Ellen passed the water to Felicity. "Oh, my goodness. Your leg!" she exclaimed as she took in the full view of the girl lying on the top bunk for the first time.

Felicity's leg was bandaged from thigh to ankle. Obviously, blood had been soaking through for some time as there was a distinct stain on the sheets around her. The young girl grabbed the water bottle, drank a large swallow and gave it back. "What happened to your leg? Are you alright?" asked Sue-Ellen.

"I'm fine, Felicity replied, "it's not hurting as much, and Stumpy brought me some pain killers yesterday. I took some last night and again this morning. I think I've stopped the bleeding now, but I haven't been able to clean up the bed. Now you go along and eat that food honey. You will need your strength."

Seemingly exhausted, the girl lay back down on her pillow and closed her eyes. "There's nothing you can do to stop them you know. I've tried everything. I cried, I screamed, I argued, I cajoled. Nothing works. The best way to deal with it all is just to switch off. Do you meditate?"

"No," Sue-Ellen answered, still trying to process all the girl had told her. "I've never really got into that stuff."

"Well, maybe now is the time to start. When they climb on top of you just close your eyes and focus on your breathing. Feel your breath coming into your body, follow it all the way in, then follow it all the way out again."

Felicity had closed her eyes now and was beginning to breathe deeply. In through her nose and out through her mouth. "It helps me. I visualise lying in a hammock, reading a book, on a lazy, summer afternoon. It takes me away from the here and now and gives me the strength to get through it. Sometimes I sing to myself. It transports me to my happy place."

"What about trying to escape?"

"Well, I thought about it the first couple of days of course.

44

I explored this room, and the bathroom, I've been over every inch of it but there doesn't seem to be any way out. The little porthole is a non-opening, re-enforced piece of glass, so that's no good. The door is bolted on the outside every time someone comes and goes. I have asked to go outside but they laughed at me. So, I gave up, there's no good living with false hope. Besides, with my leg the way it is I wouldn't be able to run, much less swim in the ocean. I'd be eaten by a shark or something. I'm going to get some rest hon. You should do the same."

Sue-Ellen returned to her bunk. She'd finished the food and the rest of the water bottle but felt restless, like she should be doing something about trying to find a way out of this situation. She waited till she could hear Felicity's breathing change as she dozed off to sleep.

Methodically she went around every inch of the walls and floor of both the cabin and the bathroom. Sadly, she had to admit that Felicity appeared to be right, there didn't seem to be a way out of the cabin other than the door. She spent the next half hour laying still on her bunk, listening to the sounds coming from outside. They were definitely at sea now. She could hear lapping water coming from low down near the floor. There were muffled footsteps occasionally, and every now and again there would be the hum of machinery - perhaps an outboard motor?

Her mind was racing. What could they want with her? She had no living relatives, no money, no rich boyfriend. A ransom wasn't going to net them anything. If they were psychopaths, well, they hadn't murdered the girls yet, so that

didn't really fit. Tossing the other girl overboard wasn't exactly murder, was it? Maybe they just wanted to keep them for sex? Although Felicity had said they had done that to them both, it obviously wasn't their main aim, as no one had done anything to them in the last day or so, that she could remember. They were being fed, given water and a bathroom. That didn't seem to follow if they were indeed sex-crazy lunatics. She couldn't understand. It was making her head hurt again so she closed her eyes and tried the deep
breathing Felicity had suggested. It must have worked, as the next time Sue-Ellen opened her eyes it was dark, and she could sense rather than hear someone in the room. The person came over to the bed and reached out to touch her.

Sue-Ellen sprang up, screaming at the man. He jumped back and hit his head on the bunk opposite.

"Oww!" he cried out, rubbing his head in pain. "You frightened me. What did you go and do that for you bitch?"

"Get away from me you beast." Sue-Ellen scrambled up the end of the bunk, making herself into a small ball, as far away from the man as she could. "Leave me alone."

"No need for yellin' woman. Ya don't want the Boss coming down here. He's drunk way too much tonight, no telling what he will want ya to do. Better off just having a kiss and cuddle with me, sweetheart." The man leered at her. She presumed he was trying to smile but because of the droopy eye and loose jowls it came out more like a lecherous grin than anything nice and friendly.

"You just leave me alone. I'll bite you. I'm not going to take this lying down you know."

The fellow they called Stumpy let out a laugh. "Oh yes, you're going to take it lying down all right, especially when the Boss comes down here." He gathered the empty food plates and went to the door, opening it and turning for one last glance at her. "Get some sleep sweetheart, you're going to need all your strength tomorrow." He disappeared through the doorway and she heard the bolt slide firmly shut.

"I told you, you should just lie there and pretend to be asleep. That's what I do," Felicity's voice drifted over in the dark. "He's not that bad, truly, he doesn't hurt you like the others. He's very gentle."

Sue-Ellen lay back down on the bunk, pulling the covers tightly around her as though adding a layer of protection would stop the unthinkable from happening. She sobbed softly and eventually fell back to sleep.

Upon waking she felt groggy. She realised her panties were missing and her arms and legs felt heavy.

"Are you ok?" Felicity asked softly.

"I think so. I feel dazed and sore, and my panties are gone." Sue-Ellen realised what must have happened and tears flooded down her cheeks.

"I'm so sorry, hon. They must have drugged the water bottles. The Boss came down here real late last night and, well, you know. I had to put up with Tank for nearly an hour. At least the Boss only lasted ten minutes. You got off lightly, I guess. I really am sorry. I've been awake a while and had a shower, so I could clean my leg. You should go clean up too if you feel up to it. They will probably bring us some food soon." Felicity's voice was calming. She appeared to have this reassuring way about her. Although what she was telling her was shocking and horrible, her voice reminded her of her real mother, many years ago, when she was a child.

Sue-Ellen didn't have very many memories of her mother but the few that remained were beautiful. They consisted mainly of those times when she would wrap her arms around her after she fell off a tricycle or had some other clumsy accident. She would rock her back and forth and sing her favourite tune. She had trouble seeing her mother's face sometimes, but her voice was embedded in Sue-Ellen's memory forever.

Sue-Ellen rose sluggishly, shuffling to the bathroom clutching her long t-shirt around her. She found her panties on the floor and brought them into the shower with her. She spent ten minutes or more scrubbing herself clean, letting the hot water run over her body and her clothes, washing the last vestiges of the men down the drain.

Finally, she stepped out of the shower, dried herself off, and put on another t-shirt from the pile folded on the shelf above the linen hamper. She wrung out her underwear and dried them with the towel. She put them back on even though they were still damp. Finding a new tooth brush and toothpaste on the hand basin she used them, and the relatively clean hair brush, to restore some semblance of normality to her appearance in the mirror. *Yes,* she thought to herself, *you are a strong woman. You can get through this. Just stay positive and use your brains to puzzle it out. You got this!*

Sue-Ellen returned to the cabin and checked in on her bunk mate. "How are you doing Felicity?" she asked, taking a quick scan of the girl's leg.

"I'm ok. I'm feeling much better, stronger and cleaner this morning. The leg seems to have taken a turn for the better, there's nowhere near as much pain as the last few days. I could even put some weight on it this morning when I went to the bathroom. I asked Stumpy for some clean sheets too. He brought me one, so I took the old ones off and I've just got a nice clean bottom sheet and a blanket on top now. How are you coping?"

She had raised herself up on her bunk now, leaning against the wall. She did appear to be much better today. Both girls looked at the door. They could hear the bolt sliding. Sue-Ellen jumped back on to her bunk as the door creaked open and bright sunlight made its way into the dark, gloomy cabin.

"Morning ladies. Hope you got a good night's sleep. We'll be docking later this afternoon and then the fun will start." Stumpy appeared very cheery this morning.

He brought in two trays, on top of each other, and had four fresh bottles of water stuffed into his jeans' pockets. He put the trays down on the shelf then handed one to Felicity. "How's that leg doing? We can't have damaged merchandise when we dock you know." Turning to hand the other tray to Sue-Ellen, he said, "How's my feisty red-head today? Well, gotta go ladies. Enjoy your lunch, drink lots of water and rest up for the party tonight." The man snickered, took the hamper from the bathroom and went out the door, sliding the bolt on the other side.

Felicity sat up on her bunk. "Do you mind passing me the food please hon?"

Sue-Ellen got up from her bunk and brought the tray to Felicity, helping her sit up across the bed and balance it on her lap. It looked like they had two rounds of sandwiches and a piece of fruit and some plain biscuits.

"Thanks, I'm starving." The girl started with the sandwich and munched down on it with vigour.

Sue-Ellen wandered back to the shelf and picked up her own tray and bottle of water, inspecting the bottle to see if the seal was still intact. It looked ok, but it was hard to tell. She erred on the side of being cautious and took the bottle to the sink in the bathroom, emptied it out and refilled it from the cold tap. "Do you want fresh water too?" she asked her bunk mate.

"Sure, thank you," Felicity answered, her mouth full of sandwich. Taking the bottles back into the room, she handed one over and then she sat on the bunk with her legs hanging over the edge.

"What do you think he meant by 'the party', and where do you think we are going to dock?" Sue Ellen enquired.

"I don't know. Maybe the crew are stopping to celebrate something, I don't know of any celebrations around here though. Perhaps we have travelled south. Isn't there some sort of Mardi Gras happening this month down south?"

"Hmm," Sue-Ellen didn't seem convinced. "Ok, so we need to have a plan then. When we arrive, and dock, they are obviously going to try to move us. They will drug us, so we will be easier for them to handle. So, what if we keep emptying out the contents, don't drink the stuff they've laced with something, but then we pretend to be drugged? We could act like we are a bit out of it, and then, when we are outside, we can wait for the right moment to make a break for it. They won't be expecting it and we can take them by surprise. We can scream and make a fuss, and hopefully we can run. What do you think?"

Felicity bent over and whispered, "Come up here and we will work on the plan."

The two women put their heads together for the next couple of hours, plotting and scheming until they were sure they had thought of every contingency. Sue-Ellen had suggested that they drink lots of water over the next few hours, so they could flush any toxins out of their bodies. They needed to be alert for their plan to work. She filled their water bottles several times. The girls lay on their bunks, trying to get some rest before they docked.

Twice over the next four hours Stumpy came in with fresh water bottles and pieces of fruit. The girls made sure to say thank you and after he left thoroughly washed the bottles out and flushed the fruit down the toilet.

As the afternoon sun began to fade through the little porthole the noise level rose from outside the door. The girls could hear some shouts and thumps, and finally the motor stopped running.

It was only ten minutes later that Stumpy and Tank came down to the bunkhouse to get the girls. Tank went to Sue-Ellen who was feigning sleep. "Come on Red, rise and shine," he cajoled her, pulling the covers off and rolling her over to the edge of the bunk. Sue-Ellen made herself go limp and spoke slowly.

"Wh-what? Wh-what is it? Where are we going?"

"We're off to see the Wizard," Tank replied with a scary smile, "The Wizard of Mexico." He laughed at his own joke.

The men manoeuvred the women to standing positions. "You sure you didn't give them too much?" Tank asked Stumpy. "The Boss won't be too happy if they can't perform tonight."

"Na, just enough. They'll be right as rain in a couple of hours," Stumpy replied as the men half dragged, half helped the girls to walk out of the bunkhouse and up the small flight of stairs to the boat deck.

Felicity kept her eyes shut against the light. Although the sun was beginning to set it was extremely bright for someone who had been below deck for the better part of ten days. Sue-Ellen pretended to be feeling a bit sick, bending over slightly and clutching her stomach. She too kept her eyes shut.

She managed to take quick peeks at her surroundings by holding her head down and away from Tank. She noticed that the marina where they had docked was nearly full, although there didn't appear to be many people around. The closest were a couple of fishermen on the next jetty. It appeared to be a deserted part of the marina, where the men were leading them down a jetty towards a parked van.

As the girls reached the end of the wooden jetty and crossed on to the cement wharf, they realised that the original plan of screaming and running from the men probably wouldn't work. The wharf was completely enclosed by six-foot razor-wire-topped fences with a manned guard booth at the gate. Sue-Ellen had no doubt that the guard would be on the boss's payroll so attracting his attention was out. She looked at Felicity as the men were distracted, talking to each other. The girl appeared dejected, shrugging her shoulders and indicating there was nothing they could do.

Right then there was a shout, followed by a big bang and a crashing noise. Everyone looked towards the crane on the next jetty. Somehow one of the ropes securing the mini-sized sea container had broken loose and the metal box had come crashing to the ground.

What happened next seemed to Sue-Ellen to take forever, and also to be over in an instant. The shout and crash had attracted the attention of people from outside the fence and across the road in an industrial area. A passing patrol car pulled up to the gate then came speeding inside to the edge of the concrete wharf.

People started running from all directions, shouting. They were indicating that the mini shipping container had spilled open upon hitting the ground and what looked like a pile of people had spilled out. They were now crying and shouting and writhing on the jetty. Some appeared injured, others were just angry. Sue-Ellen could see an opportunity. She lashed out at Tank, who barely had a grip on her arm at all, so enthralled was he by the scene unfolding in front of him. She yelled the code words to Felicity. "Hot Potato! Hot Potato!" she screamed at the top of her lungs. Felicity got the message. She stomped down on Stumpy's bad foot as hard as she could with her good leg and shoved herself away from him.

Sue-Ellen reached out and grabbed Felicity's hand, and before the men could register what was happening the girls had a healthy head start, running towards the commotion on the next jetty.

Once they realised what had happened the men gave chase, but within a few moments it was obvious they were not going to catch the girls. They slowed to a walk, so they would not arouse suspicion. The girls kept running. Seconds later they were on the edge of the crowd starting to form behind the policeman. Thinking quickly, Sue-Ellen dropped Felicity's hand and gave her a shove. She screamed and fell to the ground near the policeman's feet, grazing her leg on the wooden jetty, causing her leg to bleed profusely. Sue-Ellen immediately bent to help her, whispering, "Play along with me, play along with me." She raised her voice and cried, "Help, help us please?"

The policeman turned and rushed to Felicity's aid.

"It's ok miss. You're safe now. Those human traffickers won't escape this time. You're safe with us," he said soothingly.

Felicity smiled gratefully, and the policeman patted her hand to reassure her, but she wasn't looking at him. She was looking at her new best friend, Sue-Ellen, who had risked everything to save them. Sue-Ellen nodded at her and let the second policeman help her up.

As more police began to turn up and move the crowds back, she could see Tank and Stumpy in the distance. They started to turn away and head towards the other jetty, where the boat they had come in on was beginning to depart.

"Wait!" Sue-Ellen cried out. "They are getting away. Those two men, they were part of all this. There is another one on that blue boat there. They were all in on it! Stop them!"

* * *

Sitting in their hotel room at the airport in Tampico the girls were finally starting to feel clean. They had spent the last two days giving their statements and being praised by the local police in Ciudad Madero where their rescue had taken place.

They had both been admitted to the hospital for twenty-four hours and were sporting clean bandages. The table was piled with an assortment of creams, ointments and pain killers for their injuries. The medical staff had wanted Felicity to stay longer but she had insisted on being released with Sue-Ellen, so they could spend a couple of nights in the hotel before they flew back home. They needed some luxury, a good night's sleep, and several showers to scrub themselves clean. Neither had family or anyone special waiting for them, but they were eager to get back to their homes, none-the-less.

"What will you do when you get back?" Felicity was sitting on the balcony, sipping a tropical juice cocktail and fanning herself.

"Go back to work I guess," Sue-Ellen replied. "I bet the gang missed me at the bar."

"Yeah. I wonder if they left me off the roster?" Felicity was referring to the supermarket where she worked. It turned out that she lived only ten blocks from Sue-Ellen and she had probably served her sometime over the past two years. That supermarket was a regular shopping stop for Sue-Ellen on her way home from her gigs at a couple of the local pubs. "Pretty incredible how it all panned out." Felicity continued. "I can't believe we were nearly 1000 miles away from home. I've never been further than Houston in my life!"

"I know. Me either. Oh, no, I had to go to Tallahassee once for a wedding, when I was a kid," Sue-Ellen replied, coming back out to the balcony and taking a seat next to her new friend.

"It was damn lucky, that container breaking open like that. Those policemen could hardly believe it when we told them we didn't even come from the container like all the others – that we'd been taken in a separate kidnapping. Those other girls were lucky too. They were destined for Indonesia, the Superintendent said. He thought only about half would even have made it there alive."

"It's a shame they didn't get the Boss though," Felicity lamented.

"Yeah. But he'll get his. I'm sure of it. They are opening a whole joint task force operation now, so they will end up being able to trace him. You can't hide a distinctive boat like that for too long. That tourist got a clear photo of him too, in the background, as they were taking pictures with their smartphone." Sue-Ellen sighed. "It's certainly very beautiful here. It would have been nice to have met under better circumstances but I'm glad we did meet."

"Me too, my friend," Felicity said, raising her glass, "here's to new friends and new adventures…not quite as stressful as the last one though." The girls clinked their glasses and laughed. Felicity stood up to return to the kitchen and top up their drinks and was humming a tune to herself.

"You have a lovely voice, Felicity. I heard you singing in the shower earlier. What's the name of that song you're humming? It sounds so familiar," Sue-Ellen asked.

"It's a song my mamma used to sing to me when I was a baby," Felicity answered, a tear welling up in her eye. "Mamma died in a car crash with my daddy when I was very young. I don't know much about my real family as I was adopted when I was four. It's the only thing I remember about my mamma. I love it, it's called *Taking Pictures with my Heart*."

Victoria

The night wind softly sighed. With a heavy heart he turned, and a tear rolled down his cheek. "Sorry, Annabelle, but you are safe now. You can never hurt anyone again. I know that's all you ever wanted," he whispered. With that he lowered her gently into the hole and picked up the shovel.

It was cool, that breeze, but he was sweating slightly as he gently, even lovingly, shovelled the sand into the shallow grave. Covering her feet first, then her body, until just her head peeked out from the darkness.

"Goodbye young lady. Rest in peace now," he said as he finished his gruesome task of burying her in the lonely village graveyard, between the rose bush and the lavender plant he'd tended lovingly these past three years.

Colin's mind wandered then to a time long before he had moved here to Wales. He recalled the adventures of horseback riding over the sun-washed plains of outback Australia. He lingered over the beautiful memories of the white-water rafting in Canada, getting dunked in the icy water and laughing so much they nearly drowned. He lovingly remembered how he had held his bride while it snowed in

Central Park, New York City. They had taken a carriage ride in the freezing cold, then kept each other warm back in the hotel later that night.

Oh why, why were you taken from me so quickly, Victoria? You were put on this earth, God's great creation, just for me, but we only had two short years before he took you back to heaven with him.

Colin had asked himself this question over and over these past five years, since Victoria, his beautiful bride, had been taken from him by a car load of drunken teenagers that fateful night.

After spending the first year as a hermit, he could barely function. He ate occasionally, slept when he couldn't stay awake any longer, the ladies at the church would check on him every now and then, but mainly he would sit and gaze out at his garden and visualise his petite, blonde-haired Victoria picking roses or lavender to brighten their home.

It wasn't until the winter came that he realised he did indeed have to get his life back in order. He started walking, taking paths around the village, and everywhere he went he was reminded of his wife. Passing the school, he'd remember how they had talked of raising a family here. Pausing in front of the house where she grew up.

Finally, the second year, he made a decision. He'd put the house on the market and move to a new place. With Victoria's ashes, in a beautiful urn, he would start over, somewhere new. Life could begin again. He'd take his happy memories to keep him company and refuse to be tormented by everything he saw around him, reminding him of what could have been.

So, he moved to Wales. He found a little place high up on the cliffs where he could sit on his verandah and gaze out across the sea towards Ireland. Taking his coffee and settling into a love swing he built, he'd watch the gulls swoop and glide. His mind wandering to love lost and missed opportunities, but he was content to sit in this forlorn place and recall the beautiful memories he had stored in his head.

Colin had secured employment as soon as he arrived. He wasn't a wealthy man. Although his needs were modest, he desired to work, at least part-time, to live out his life here in this peaceful, if secluded place.

He had his dad's trade, handed down over generations, and was an excellent tailor, although there was not much call for that sort of work here in the country, so he utilised his skills in a different way. The local fishing industry was extremely grateful to have a local person repair their fishing nets so quickly and with such skill.

Until Colin arrived they had sent their nets over fifty miles to the nearest city to have them repaired. He managed to secure enough work to commit to two days per week. Barton's Bait and Tackle had set him up in a corner of their boat repair workshop with some good quality machinery for a small percentage of what he charged the local fisherman. They were excited to offer this new service to their clientele and, truth be known, they were also happy that Colin kept himself to himself, just a short greeting in the morning and a farewell at night.

Old Ewan Barton was not one for chit-chat and time wastin' as he put it. He would doff his cap in the morning and more often than not just grunt as Colin left for the day. A comfortable arrangement for both men.

His second job, half a day doing landscape gardening for the council, didn't pay much, but he enjoyed working with the flowers in the beautiful memorial gardens. It reminded him of the garden Victoria had planted at their home years ago.

Colin spent his spare time on the beach. He would walk, rummage for flotsam and jetsam, he collected shells and generally enjoyed the fresh sea air. He didn't particularly like the sea, not to sail on or swim in, but he enjoyed its company. It kept up a comfortable hum in the background, so you knew it was there, but it never expected him to talk back. At times it got into a foul mood, waves crashing to the shore, orchestrating a cacophony of thunderous sound... but that too suited Colin. He sometimes felt like that inside.

It began around the third anniversary of Victoria's death. Colin started hearing voices. The first few times he thought he must have dozed off, out on the love seat. He presumed he was having a vivid dream.

After a few weeks of this he realised that these intermittent voices were unquestionably occurring while he was awake. They were mumbling and what they were saying was garbled most of the time, the volume too low to make out distinct words.

He began to listen more intently. Concentrating on distinguishing words, then sentences. After a month or so he began to keep a journal. He was interested in what the voices had to say, writing everything down, using a different colour pen for each voice. It was as if he was privy to some private conversation between two people, perhaps having a disagreement or discussion on the other side of a hedge. He likened the idea to eavesdropping, you couldn't see them, but you knew they were there and could vaguely make out what they were saying.

After nearly a year the voices started asking questions. Things like 'why?' Why did the innocent have to die? Why wasn't the court system stricter with people who offended or broke the law? Why was life not fair? Wasn't it God's law that said, 'an eye for an eye'?

Over the ensuing months the questions became more specific. Why did those teenagers get off so lightly? Losing their licence and serving only twelve weeks in jail.

For taking someone's life? Was that fair? Was that just? What right did they have, not only to take Victoria's life, but to ruin Colin's too? They had probably done worse things since then. Maybe they were just evil people?

The voices became more insistent. They would not let him rest. They began to talk to him constantly, at his work, while he walked on the shore, even in his dreams now.

They convinced him that justice really hadn't been served in this case. Those girls were living complete, happy lives while his Victoria sat in an urn on the mantelpiece. She was unable to fulfil her dreams of raising a family, eventually watching her children grow and marry, and would never be able to enjoy her grandchildren in her golden years. No, fate had not dealt the hand fairly in this situation. The cards had most certainly been stacked in those teenagers' favour and against the innocent parties.

Colin hadn't been interested in following the case particularly at the time. He knew that the girls were all local, the three of them, Trish, Marie and Annabelle.

The voices now directed him to do something. Four years had passed since Victoria had died. It was time he stood up for what was right and just, and he began an investigation to track down the girls.

Trish was first. It wasn't difficult as her surname was Frederickson and in the small village where they had lived her father had been the one and only judge. Colin soon discovered that Patricia June Frederickson had died of a drug overdose just one year after the accident. There had been a half page story in the local paper about how drugs were on the rise in the town. For a few days Colin absorbed the information and the voices decided that this was probably a fitting end to that wasted life.

Marie was a little more difficult to track down. As he didn't have a computer, Colin would travel into town and use the free one in the little library set up inside an ante-room, located on the side of the council office. Over the weeks he came to know the little grey-haired old lady who manned the front desk.

She would see him coming and set up the internet for him, usually stopping to chat for a few moments. One day she asked him what it was he was researching, and he told her he was looking up a couple of distant relatives that he had lost touch with over the years. One afternoon, when it was quiet, she sat and helped him by showing him how to look up public records, reverse telephone directories, even a genealogy site. This was much appreciated as it was only a week after that he discovered that Marie Fahey was serving twenty years in a state prison for murdering her abusive husband in an alcohol-fuelled rage.

After a long discussion that evening he agreed with the voices. It appeared fate had finally caught up with Marie and they were all satisfied with the final punishment dished out to the girl who was part of the trio who stole Colin's wife from him.

By the end of the following year he was ready to tackle Annabelle, the driver of the vehicle that had mowed down Victoria, the innocent pedestrian making her way home from book club that night. After nearly three weeks of investigation, and a little extra help from Mavis, the librarian, Colin found young Annabelle.

She was currently ensconced in a rehabilitation facility in northern England, not too far from the Welsh border. It appeared that Annabelle had spent the past three years in and out of rehab, either pressured by her father, who was a high-ranking police officer, or court ordered, following the nineteen drink-driving offences with which she had been charged.

Two weeks ago, he had made the trip to the town and scoped out the location, the buildings and the procedure.

Although Annabelle was there as a self-admitted patient this time, there was still a front desk and sign-out sheet that had to be used. He had arranged a tour of the facility under the presumption he had a nephew who may want to check-in.

It hadn't been difficult to gather information on where Annabelle was accommodated, and he had made mental notes about everything as a chatty young nurse escorted him on his tour. He paid particular attention when she had entered the security code to the outer hallway door and to the kitchen entrance. He had been emphatic about the kitchen being included on the tour, weaving a tale of his nephew's culinary skills and appreciation of food.

Last Tuesday, late at night, he'd gone back and parked around the corner from the back entrance in the alley, where there were no security cameras. He'd dressed in black and it had taken only a couple of minutes to let himself in through the kitchen entrance. He had used the cleaners' corridor to make his way to Annabelle's room and, while she slept soundly on sleeping pills, he gave her another sedative. He gathered her in the blanket he had brought with him and let himself out.

The only camera inside this wing was at the opposite end of the hallway. It covered half of the doors to the rooms, but not Annabelle's, and its orientation was to serve its main purpose - to watch patients entering the mess hall attached to the kitchen. He had loaded his cargo into the boot of the car and driven back to his home on the cliff.

For the next two days he kept Annabelle sedated, not enough that she was completely out of it, but enough to ensure she would remain calm and controllable. He spent Tuesday and Wednesday lecturing her, making her fully aware of the consequences of her actions five years ago. She would murmur, nod her head in acquiescence, as though she fully understood the error of her ways and the repercussions of her actions that night.

The voices had directed him to just throw her off the cliff, but he had also heard from Victoria these past few days. He had heard her saying she understood where he was coming from, how she knew he was only about getting justice for her and that she knew how much he was hurting. However, she could not condone him throwing this girl hundreds of feet over the cliff to her death on the rocks below.

He knew she was right, of course. Although his heart longed for a punishment to suit the crime, he had never agreed with capital punishment. He had never been a violent man and as such was quite prepared to just make sure she knew the error of her ways. He would teach her how important it was to turn herself around, steer away from the evil alcohol that was ruining her life, and perhaps convince her to make amends by volunteering at a hospital, where she would see firsthand the results of drink-driving and the suffering of those left behind.

On Thursday morning he felt he had made some headway and lowered the dose of the sedative. By Thursday afternoon Annabelle was sitting up, restrained of course, but able to communicate with him. He spent time carefully going over all the facts again, clearly outlining the situation and she appeared to comprehend and even agree.

She told him Friday morning that she was experiencing regret. That she felt she should seek penance by doing as he suggested, enrolling in a volunteer program at the local hospital. Colin was impressed at how intelligent the girl was, without the alcohol she could essentially end up being a valuable contributor to society.

They spent Friday afternoon talking, like old friends, and on Saturday he felt that she had truly had a revelation. Colin let her walk around the house, stretching her legs and attending to her personal needs. Although he had secured the restraints before he went to bed, he was sure that once they sat down and worked out a plan for her over the next couple of days, she would be ready to start her new life, participating in her community as she should, perhaps even campaigning against drink-driving, one of the issues they had discussed at length.

Colin slept well that night. He didn't hear the voices, even Victoria let him sleep through the night. He awoke refreshed and revitalised.

"Morning," he called cheerily to Annabelle who was waking on the cot in the sitting room. "Would you like breakfast?"

"Yes please. I'm starving this morning. It must be due to all those awful toxins having left my body. I think I am starting to feel normal again."

He was very glad to hear that, and she even looked brighter and more cheerful today.

"Hey, why don't I get you breakfast for a change Colin? You have done so much for me, it's the least I could do to start repaying you, and 'paying it forward' as you so aptly put it." Annabelle had sat on the edge of her cot, swinging her legs over the side, the handcuffs still secured to a chain which wound around the pot belly stove.

He thought this might be the perfect opportunity for her to ease into thinking about others before herself for a change.

"Sure, that would be lovely Annabelle. Let me get those cuffs off, I know I can trust you to do the right thing, can't I?"

"Of course. You are an intelligent man, Colin, with a good heart. I can see now that all I needed was someone like you to come along and take my hand and guide me down the right path. Would you like eggs and bacon? Some toast?" she rubbed her wrists as he released the cuffs.

"That would be lovely. I will put the kettle on for us and make some tea."

Annabelle busied herself preparing breakfast. She peered into cupboards, looking for plates and utensils. Obviously quite adept in the kitchen, she soon had bacon frying, eggs poaching and bread toasting.

Colin took a seat at the table and glanced through the paper from yesterday. Annabelle came over and set the table with plates and condiments and returned with the frypan to dish the bacon. Just as she drew up to the table the tongs slipped from her grasp and clattered to the floor.

Instinct kicked in and Colin leant down and reached under the table for them. As he began to rise with the tongs she brought the full force of the hot frying pan straight down on his head. She let go and it crashed to the floor.

"Arrgghh, dammit!" Colin shouted. Luckily for him the pan had caught the edge of the table as she brought it down and that had reduced the blow to about half the speed and force. He staggered forward, into the table, as she headed straight for the front door. She struggled with the latch, but he had cautiously locked the deadbolt with the key from the inside before retiring to bed the previous night, taking the key to his bedside table. Annabelle screamed with frustration, crying out for help. She knew it was helpless, he had explained in the beginning that they were located on a tiny property, on a cliff, outside the remote village in Wales.

There was no one around to hear her or to come to her aid. She turned to her captor, ready to defend herself against an attack. But no attack came. Colin was calm, he had blood dripping from a cut above his eye but there was no malice on his face. He walked over to Annabelle and reached out and gently clasped her hand. She was stunned. She meekly followed as he led her back to the cot and the handcuffs. She lay on the bed and cried.

Colin took his time in the bathroom, cleaning up his bloodied head. He took two headache tablets and put his shirt into cold water, so that the blood stain wouldn't set.

As he withdrew the vial of liquid from the medicine cabinet, a sigh of sadness escaped his lips. It didn't take long after the injection for Annabelle to slip into a coma.

As soon as she was out he gave her the lethal dose and put on his old gardening clothes. Later that evening he made the trip to his memorial garden in the village. It took time, but he gave her a proper resting place, and as he finished up and returned his tools to the council's gardening shed he sighed and muttered.

"I wish it could have turned out differently. I sincerely do." The voices and Victoria agreed. He returned to his car and picked up the urn he'd brought with him from the mantlepiece.

"Here you go my sweet Victoria. It's time now for you to find your final resting place." He spread the ashes over Annabelle's freshly dug grave and around the roses and lavender. He continued to speak to his beloved as he sprinkled, "Watch over Annabelle and Patricia up in heaven. Marie too, when she arrives. I know you forgive them, even if I don't. Goodbye my love." The voices were finally silent.

Kitty

He usually waited till night-fall. That's when you could get the pick of the crop. However, these past few days the hunger had been gnawing away at him. The weather had turned cold. He needed to snuggle. He needed someone new to hold him. He had to have some company. NOW.

Charlie looked up and down the street and spied a woman hunched over in a doorway. She was wearing a familiar scarf, one he'd seen around here many times over the past month or so. He motioned for her to come over.

"$50 buddy, or $80 if you want the lot." She kept looking up and down the street as she spoke with him.

"That's a little steep isn't it?" he asked her through the open car window.

"I'm freezing my fanny off here so I'm not taking my clothes off for anything less."

He didn't recall her face, but it was obvious she'd been on the game for a long time. She looked old and tired, her hair slightly matted, and she had that weather-beaten look of street people. He remembered the scarf, and now she was closer he thought he recognised her from the block up near the deli.

"Is this your usual corner?" he enquired.

"Nope, I usually work the next block but there's no protection there from this damn wind. Now are we going to stand around and chat all day or are you looking for some company handsome?"

Yes, straight down to business. She was certainly an experienced hooker.

"Sure, come on in. I'll take the lot," Charlie said, unlocking the door and waiting till she had belted herself in before taking off.

He headed across Dover Ave and past the stadium to his home on the edge of the industrial area. The woman sat in silence, chewing gum and gazing out the window.

"My place is just two blocks further. Are you warm enough? I can turn up the heat if you like," he asked his passenger.

"Nope, I'm fine," she replied, tightening her coat a little around her shoulders.

They pulled up into his driveway. Charlie got out to come around and open the door, but she had already climbed out by the time he got there. He doubted she even realised he'd made the effort. Women like her were not used to the niceties of life. He led the way up the little path to the porch, unlocked the door, then held it open for her. Once inside he bolted the door. Taking her coat and scarf, he said, "You go ahead, into the front room, where it's warm. Take a seat and relax while I pour us a couple of drinks."

He emptied some cheap red wine into the glasses and added a dash of something special to hers. Entering the small loungeroom he noticed she was looking at his collection of rare medical books and the shelf of accounting manuals in the bookcase.

"I love to read. Do you?" he asked her.

"Yeah, I read a bit. Mainly Vogue and Time magazine, coz that's what the rich folk throw out in the garbage," she cackled, and took the wine. "Thanks. So, let's get down to business handsome. What's your name?"

"Charles, but you can call me Charlie," he replied.

"Ok Charlie, it's $80 for the lot, unless you want something special, then we can negotiate," she cackled again.

"No problem, let's make it $100 and see what happens," Charlie replied.

She made her way over to him, sat on the sofa and placed her glass on the side table. She started to undo a couple of buttons.

"No rush, honey. Let's finish our wine before we get down to business. This will get us nice and warm," he insisted, picking up the glass and handing it to her. "We can get romantic a little later, drink up first."

The woman moved closer, rubbing her hand along his thigh. He got out his wallet and removed two fifties to pay her, unaware that she had put down her glass once more. "Right then big boy, let's get started."

It was at that moment, as soon as the code words *Big Boy* had been uttered, that the door flew open and members of the vice squad came bursting into the room.

"Hands where I can see them!" "Hands on your head!" "Don't move!" voices shouted at him from all directions.

"Charles Smith, you're under arrest for solicitation of prostitution. Stand up. You are being taken to Cannington Police Station for questioning. You are not obliged to say or do anything unless you wish to do so, but whatever you say or do may be used in evidence. Do you understand?" The police officer handcuffed him and marched him out to the paddy wagon parked on the street. The four other officers congratulated Senior Constable Georgia Holstein who had been under cover for two weeks and had managed to round up twenty-one johns in *Downtown Clean-up*.

The project had been under way for nearly three months now. The vice squad, along with officers from Cannington, Victoria Park and Belmont had organised a task force and worked hand in hand on this undercover operation. Between them, the forty-two officers involved had collared over three hundred johns, thirty-four pimps and madams. They had also taken possession of large quantities of meth, heroin and cocaine. Added to the twelve semi-automatic weapons and fifty-three hand guns they had confiscated this was turning out to be a very profitable joint venture for the Western Australia Police Commissioner.

The whole operation had been the brain child of Superintendent Crompton, who headed up the South Metropolitan division of vice. It had come about due to his love of the old downtown area, where he had grown up as a child, playing in local parks, attending basketball training and church on Sundays. He had lobbied for over a year for funds, time and manpower to undertake one of the biggest clean-up operations this city had seen in years.

As they were leaving Senior Constable Holstein spied a cat bowl on the floor of the kitchen. Being an animal lover from an early age, she told the others to go ahead, she would quickly check and make sure the cat had food before they left. She went into the kitchen, opened a couple of cupboards and found, to her surprise, three entire cupboards stacked with dry cat food.

Pouring some into the bowl the police officer was puzzled, asking herself why someone would buy such large quantities of cat food, when she hadn't even seen a cat in the house.

As she turned to leave, she heard it. A tiny, mewing sound. It appeared to be coming from the behind the door of the pantry cupboard in the corner. She opened the door gently and could hear the noise a little louder, although she could not see any kittens.

"C'mon baby, where are you?" she called quietly. "Puss, Puss, Puss."

The mewing sound got slightly louder and she ventured a little further into the pantry. Georgia leant on a shelf to bend down and peer along the floor, and to her surprise the shelf completely gave way. It appeared to spring open and she staggered forward. The shelf, and the others above it, had swung inwards. It appeared to be a concealed door and she was now faced with a set of stairs that disappeared downwards, presumably to a wine cellar.

As she was made up to look like an old hooker, dressed in undercover clothes, Georgia did not have her torch and other standard issue police equipment, with her, so she ventured forward tentatively.

"Here kitty, kitty, kitty," she called softly. The police officer hesitantly descended the first three steps and noticed a pull string suspended from the ceiling.

She tugged it to turn on the light and the huge room in front of her was flooded with bright white. In contrast to the older, tired décor of the rooms above, it was a spotlessly clean environment. Everything was white and shiny. The sink and floor had been polished till they shone. There were all types of equipment stored in organised metal shelving racks and it took her a full minute to realise what it was that she had discovered.

This was some sort of underground medical theatre room. It had a gurney in the middle and a ceiling-mounted light system, racks of tools and glass fridges with what looked like rows of medicines and blood pouches for transfusions.

Her hand flew to her mouth as she turned towards the other side of the room where there were two metal cages. They were not unlike those at the Shenton Park dog pound where she had helped her father, a local vet, when she was a teenager.

However, these cages were slightly bigger, and they each held a camp stretcher, a steel bucket, and a large plastic cat bowl. Each contained a person curled up, asleep or drugged. One woman looked as though she might be dead, the other was crying and making a mewing sound…that had been what Georgia had heard from upstairs. "Oh my God!" she exclaimed. The police officer turned to shout up the stairs. "Help, help me please? Down here, through the kitchen."

She ran to the cages to help the women. She spied an old-fashioned ring of keys on a hook on the far wall and hastily tried opening the door to the cage of the woman who was crying.

"It's ok, hon, you're ok," Georgia spoke reassuringly, "We are here to help you. He's gone now. You are safe."

She yanked the door open and proceeded to unlock the next cage. Footsteps sounded on the stairs behind her and the room was suddenly echoing with people's voices, shouting and calling for assistance.

"Oh my God!" "Bloody hell! What the…" "Damn, what the hell is going on here?" The last was the voice of her Sergeant who had obviously come back into the building to find her or had heard her cries for help.

Two ambulances took the women off to Royal Perth Hospital and police officer Holstein was checked over in the emergency department. Georgia was told later that day that the first woman, Lilliana, the one she had heard crying from the pantry, would make a full recovery. She would remain in hospital for a couple of days on fluids and being treated for shock. The second woman, a backpacker named Heidi, was not dead as they had first thought, but had been very near to it. She had passed into a diabetic coma due to not being given food or insulin. The paramedics had quickly got her to intensive care and she made a full recovery over the following weeks.

* * *

During the next few months it came to light that Charles

Smith had been picking up women from the streets for well over four years. He'd taken them home under the guise of paying them for sex. After having his way with them and torturing them in this room he would dismember them, then dispose of their bodies in a huge vat of lye, aka sodium hydroxide. This would reduce the bodies to virtually nothing – some water-soluble salts and liquids, which he could flush down the industrial drains he had installed in his underground lab. They had found traces of twenty-one different individuals, many of whom would sadly never be identified.

Investigators believed Charles life had taken a turn for the worse when he had lost his highly paid accounting job due to the Global Financial Crisis. His wife had left him three years ago, citing his alcoholism and resulting bad temper as the reason for divorce. She had taken his two children back to Denmark to live with her family. Charles had eventually lost his big, family home, in a lush garden estate and been forced to rent a small, one-bedroom cottage, not far from the industrial area.

After nearly three years being unemployed he'd finally managed to secure a poorly paid, casual security guard position, for a local car dealer. His wife had communicated that she had always believed he had a mean streak in him, perhaps from the abuse he suffered, at the hands of his drunken father, as a child. She had filed four domestic violence reports over the three months prior to her leaving him to move to Copenhagen.

Senior Constable Holstein and the team of four from the Belmont police station received commendations for their exceptional service on this operation. Lieutenant Crompton was promoted, and the entire project was written up as a successful venture. So successful in fact that it was used as an example to train new recruits in the art of being vigilant and to listen and take note of even the smallest things that appear out of place in a particular situation.

Georgia went on two weeks' leave not long after the case was closed, and the paperwork finished. She needed to take time out to reflect on her own life. Working undercover took its toll on many police officers and it was important that they stay grounded in their own, real life.

Thinking about her own personal situation she decided that there was something missing. She needed something or someone to come home to each day, someone to shower love and affection on, amid this tough, often gut-wrenching job. She brought home her new kitten on the second day of her leave and she named it Lilliana. Lilly for short.

Village Life

Late in July the women and older children were sent out to gather reeds and high grasses for thatch. The men would be returning soon from their three-week hunting trip, and then the women of a certain age would fall pregnant, so new homes would be required as the tribe expanded.

This had gone on for centuries and as Nafula sat in the hot African sun she contemplated the serene and still grass plains, with the mountains in the distance. Idyllic. That is how most people would describe it. No telephones. No televisions. No electricity. This was not a society who fretted about Facebook posts, deadlines or the latest fashion trends. No commuter rush or hectic schedules here. Just the business of living. Of enjoying the simple, back-to-nature, style of village life. Sitting by the fire with the elders, recounting stories of tribes long gone, of their forefathers and their forays into the distant mountains.

However, Nafula knew that while this is what the outside world would see if they 'looked in' on the village, reality was not nearly as pleasant. Underneath this seemingly harmonious, peaceful exterior, these women endured atrocities most people would never encounter. Rape was a common occurrence. Incest was rife. Once a girl turned twelve in this tribe she was passed from family to family, sometimes referred to as a *rite of passage,* similar to the ancient traditions of *first night* or other ceremonial rituals that had long since died out in civilised cultures. By fourteen the girl would be promised to a man from this, or a nearby tribe, and married off, for a price of course, so she could start rearing children of her own. Those slightly stronger women, like Nafula, the ones who might complain or make a fuss, endured beatings and punishments too horrible to describe. Nafula had been sent away by her father at the age of ten, for three years, to get educated at a nearby town due to her strong will and frequent complaints about the treatment of some of her friends.

The youngest of the boys would sometimes suffer abuse too, if their fathers were that way inclined, or the barter price was high enough. She would hear the mothers sobbing quietly late at night, and she would often see the bruises or resultant broken bones. The resident medic – a volunteer from Médecins Sans Frontières (MSF, or doctors without borders as it was more commonly known), was continually kept busy. Always very low key, no big bandages, or splints. There could be no visible signs, the elders would not tolerate that. Usually a tight compress of rags or cloths with ointment and antibiotics was all that was required. If more severe first aid needed to be administered the child would be shipped off to the small hospital, sixty kilometres away, for a few days recovery.

Nafula's education in the city had taught her much more than she, or indeed her family, had expected. His daughter had become wise in a way that her father did not approve of. She was now acutely aware that drugs ran rampant in the village. The men abusing them to get high, so they could get the most out of their sexual experiences. The women took them to survive their life. Uppers to mask their tiredness, sorrow and pain, Valium to forget. They would sometimes give small doses to their children, mixed in with their food, to help them through the abuse, or the beatings. Nafula often spent her time counselling these girls in private.

Alcohol was also used – although because the tribal elders received extra government funding for labelling themselves a 'dry' community the alcohol needed to be brought in secretly, often disguised in supplies. This wasn't difficult. There weren't any government employees that remained in the community permanently. They came and went, as the political parties of the day saw fit to fund them for various projects. From her conversations with the visiting nurses, Nafula was aware that alcohol abuse was a constant and topical issue. Once she made friends with a student doctor who had stayed for a week and sadly, she now knew, that the rate of Foetal Alcohol Syndrome Disorder in this part of her country, was one of the world's highest.

Most aid workers would arrive with supplies, and they might also bring a teacher, to instruct the children, or train the youth how to build better shelters. Nafula's tribe had survived here on this plain for centuries, so how these people, who lived in huge cities, on the other side of the country, could begin to know better than the elders, Nafula could not fathom. Mostly they were ok though. They would provide new equipment like water filtration kits or medical supplies. Sometimes they brought paper, books and writing materials which were wonderful for the small children to experience.

One lady got funding for three pull carts and some saws and scythes. This had made the women's grass and reed gathering much easier. They were able to drag the carts down to spots by the river where the best high grasses grew and drag them back to the village fully laden. It saved the women carrying such heavy loads. It meant fewer trips and much less strain on their backs. That didn't last long. The men soon commandeered the carts and used them for their own purposes, breaking one of them not long after the lady left the village.

Nafula broke free from her day dreaming as she smelt the strong, pungent odour of smoke. Jumping to her feet, she looked in all directions to find the source of such an acrid smell. It appeared to be coming from three or four kilometres away to the north. There was a small black plume rising towards the sky. It was probably nothing, but if that hot wind was coming in this direction then it could turn into an issue soon. She spied a cackle of hyenas heading away from where the smoke appeared to originate.

Nafula, who's name meant being born in the rainy season, of which there was very little in these parts, thought she had better return to check on her son. She had left him in his reed basket covered with fine woven netting, asleep in her hut. He would be due for a feed soon and she could check with the women about the smoke while she was there. She adored her baby son, Isaac. He was the reason she got up in the morning, the reason she endured living in this village, putting up with her husband Ommar.

Her husband was nowhere near as rough or abusive as others in the tribe. Ommar was the first-born son of the respected tribal elder Chiamaka. Chiamaka had been the most revered of all religious leaders of this tribe for nearly eight decades. Ommar's father was just twenty years old when he began holding worship services on a weekly basis. He had arrived with his family from the other side of the mountain and over time earned the respect of the tribe. He would travel on missions into the barren wasteland, bringing back lost souls whom the tribe would welcome, then put to work in the village. His first-born son, Ommar, was being groomed to take over from his father, learning his ways for more than three years now. His father had instilled in him the virtues of loving all people, respecting women, a firm belief in the higher powers. Ommar had learned much from him. Nafula and Ommar had cared for the old man for the last four years, since Chiamaka's wife had passed on. Chiamaka's other son, Wafiq, had left the tribe many years ago to pursue a life in the city, turning against his father's beliefs and joining the gun runners and arms dealers that ran rife there.

Nufula didn't mind caring for the old man. He had always been kind to her and it was as if she had two small children to care for. She would feed him ground meal, wash his face, read to him and sing to him, as she would to Isaac. They both always seemed to love it when she sang.

As she got closer to the village she was aware of a rising hum, unusual as the men had not yet returned from their hunting expedition. She quickened her pace and was frightened to see women rushing across the central square, carrying blankets and baskets.

"What is it Jabulela?" she asked her neighbour, a young girl of about twenty who had three little children, "what is happening here?"

"It is fire Nufula, fire is coming. It has burned hundreds of kilometres of land and taken two villages to the north. It is heading this way. Ruth has instructed us all to take what we can carry, bring the children and go to the ceremonial area on the other side of the river. The fire will not get us there. We will be safe. You must hurry. Get Isaac and go now!" The girl was nearly hysterical and ran off to gather more goods and her children.

If Ruth has instructed them then it must be so. Ruth was Chiamaka's younger sister and the unofficial leader of the tribal women. Women have no official leaders, not in this tribe, but they have all looked to the wisdom and guidance of Ruth for years. She has handed down skills to generations of girls, helped raise many children, some of whom became orphans during the last upheaval, and the last famine.

Ruth was wise, and the women of the tribe respected her and looked to her for leadership when needed. Nufula was confused - did she go to Ruth's hut and gather more information, or did she head straight for her home to grab Isaac and Chiamaka? She turned left and ran directly towards the elders' section of camp. Ruth lived there with her invalid husband, four daughters, and their families, in the first three huts in the camp. She had earned her place there, even as a woman, although the tribe would say it was because of her husband's heroic efforts in the great upheaval, the valiant rescue of the tribal leaders and his personal record of slaying over thirty invaders. Her husband had become bedridden a few years ago and she looked after him there and helped her daughters raise their families.

"Ruth! Ruth!" Nufula shouted as she ran up to the first hut.

There was no answer, and no-one inside. She moved on to the second. "Ruth?"

"Yes, my child," Ruth's calming tone was reassuring to Nufula.

"Is it true Ruth? Is there a fire? Do we have to go?" there was panic in her voice now.

"Yes Nufula. You must get Isaac and gather your possessions. I have sent my daughter to get Chiamaka prepared. We will take him with us, you have enough to worry about with Isaac. Go now, hurry, but do not panic. It will be all right. Our God is looking down upon us, child. Go!" She kissed the top of the girl's head and pushed her off in the direction of her hut.

Nufula ran then. She ran like the very devil was chasing her. She got to her hut and found Ruth's youngest daughter packing items into two large baskets. She ran to Isaac's basket and saw that he was starting to stir. She began to sing his favourite lullaby while gathering her precious possessions and putting them in a colourful backpack retained from her schooling days. She gathered the framed photograph of her family, her mother's crucifix, her sister's bracelet and some trinkets she had salvaged from their hut during the great upheaval.

She then stuffed Isaac's possessions into one large basket. She gathered Ommar's precious items and put them in too. The second basket she filled with food, water, medical supplies and other items she might need.

She checked on Chiamaka who appeared to be safe on the cart Ruth's daughter had secured. She tied a basket to the back of the cart and filled it quickly with Chiamaka's bible and his few items of clothes. On top she put his wife's special blanket which she had made for them when they married. Nufula then gathered her two baskets, put on her backpack, and picked up Isaac in his sleeping basket. She attached the straps and mounted that to her chest. Ruth's daughter nodded to her, indicating she should go, so with a quick, wistful glance around her hut she whispered a tiny prayer then left.

Outside Nufula found Jabulela and her children standing in the square. The girl was laden with baskets and was trying to keep the children close while attempting to assemble her drag cart. Nufula put her baskets down, assembled the drag cart and together the two girls loaded all their baskets on to it, securing them and topping it all off with three big blankets.

Nufula tied a rope around the whole thing and placed the two smallest children on top of the blankets. She slipped their feet under the rope and told them to hang on to the rope like they were big boys riding a goat! They giggled and held on for their dear lives.

Now that she had only Isaac and her backpack to carry, she was able to take the other side of the pull cart, and between them the girls dragged their load towards the river, the third child mounted on Jabulela's shoulders.

Once the group was underway they were able to pick up speed and soon joined many other women with their children and elders who were headed in the same direction. It did not take long to reach the river, but by the time the girls got there they could hear the fire, in the distance. They could see smoke, heavy and thick, and hear animals squealing now.

There was a buddy system working at the river. The six rafts owned by the village were taking people, carts and belongings to the other side, the ropes being pulled on each side by the strongest women, and a few of the boys who had been too young to accompany the men on the hunt. They were making quick work of getting the groups across, so it only took a short time for the girls to get their belongings and their children to the other side. Once they were there Nufula told Jabulela to stay and help the next couple of rafts. She would take the children and the cart to safety behind the ridge of sand and rocks on the edge of the mountain range. It was a struggle, but a young lad from the elder's camp offered to help pull the cart, so they managed.

At the makeshift refuge the villagers had set up, the older women had already organised basic shelter with tents strung between trees and blankets forming lean-to's. There was a fire, water was boiling, and food was being made for the children. Nufula organised an area for herself, Isaac, Jabulela and her three children.

She arranged two blankets on the ground and told all the children it was an island, in a big sea, and if they stayed on the island, playing quietly, she'd make them a very special dinner tonight. She sat then and held Isaac.

He had been such a good boy, not objecting once that he had not yet been fed. Nafula changed him, fed him and cuddled him, cooing soft lullaby's so that he would not be frightened. Jabulela joined them after a short time and the girls prepared an early meal for the children, wiped their faces and soon had them lying on the blankets, heads curled in the young mothers' laps.

All through the night the women stayed in their refuge. They helped each other to feed and look after the children, the sick and the frail. They sung folk songs around the campfire to ward off the bad spirits associated with bushfires, and they prayed that the river would keep them safe.

By morning the air was thick and fetid but the heat they had felt the night before had dissipated. A small group of women went on a foray to the river to assess the situation and returned after just fifteen minutes to inform the villagers that the river had indeed protected them, and whilst it did not look pretty on the other side, it did appear that the fire had burned out during the night.

The older women of the tribe decided that it would be safer to stay one more night where they were, and in the morning, they would send a small team to assess the damage to the village. The girls spent the day amusing the children, Nufula helped care for Chiamaka and Ruth's husband, and then settled down for another evening in the bush.

Although she felt safe and thankful for being spared by the fire, Nufula couldn't help but feel sad too, for the loss of the village that had been her home for nearly seventeen years.

The next morning the advance team set off at dawn and by lunchtime they were back.

They were excited, and jubilant shouts woke Nufula out of her dozing, Isaac curled in her lap.

"What is it Jabulela? What has happened?" she asked the young girl who was running back to their blanket.

"It's a miracle Nufula!" the girl was breathless. "The men. They made it back in advance of the fire and formed a human water chain and doused the entire village with river water before the fire could get there. The village. It's saved! The only thing burned were the animal shelters outside the village fence…but they freed the animals, so none of them were lost either!"

Jabulela flung herself down on the blanket and threw her arms around Nufula, and the children, not really understanding what was happening, sensed the elation and joined in. The two girls and their families hugged, then started collecting their belongings. They made their way slowly back across the river. It was early afternoon before they finally walked back in to their village.

The buildings were dirty and wet, covered with ash and smelled of smoke. Nufula carried Isaac in his basket, and as she entered the square she saw Ommar coming from their hut, their home, that he had saved for his family. He was covered with soot and ash and had blood coming from gashes down the side of his face, but she ran to him and let him scoop her up into his arms. It was at that moment that she knew…there was no other place in the world she would rather be than in her husband's arms, in her village, her home.

Burlap Sacks

Pensively she let go of the bars and turned away from the window; anxiety, dread, fear, all these emotions were intermingled as they flowed through her. What would it be this time? A girl? A boy? A couple?

She straightened the home-made cushions, unconsciously keeping vigilant for the sound of the car in the drive. Yes, there it was, the rumble of the garage door opening, the squeak of the brakes on the old Ford pickup as it crawled up the driveway and into the gloomy garage. She hurried to the connecting door, opening it with a sense of foreboding.

He was excited, you could see it on his face. He used to look like that when he came home to *her*. There was a time when she was the cause of that smile, that excitement. When had they drifted apart, she wondered. When was the point where he had to turn to other pursuits to get that same feeling? That happiness? That pleasure?

It had been going on for over a year now, here in Mountville. At first it had been intermittent, he brought home the first few over a period of nearly four months, but now it was weekly, in fact, only six days since the last one!

She can remember the first time, like it was yesterday. Her feelings of shame at his bringing home a girl for a 'threesome'. Brandon, her devoted husband, had taken it upon himself to 'spice up their love life' as he put it. She had endured the embarrassment, but as she realised that the girl was not actually a willing participant, and was indeed drugged, she had been overcome with revulsion for the man she had married. After an entire evening of sex, he had taken an old iron pot to the back of the girl's head, knocking her unconscious. In the morning when he awoke he decided that there was no other solution than to kill the girl and dispose of her body.

After the first two girls, he had the furnace in the basement upgraded, making it a little easier for the body disposal, but the actual clean-up had taken a long time back then. Now they were on their fifteenth or sixteenth, no, come to think of it - it was their nineteenth victim, and she had that part of it down to a fine art.

At least she didn't have to participate anymore, and these past few months he had stopped demanding that she watch too. *Thank God for small mercies*, she told herself.

Quickly she donned the plastic apron, shower hat and disposable gloves she kept in the basket by the garage door.

"Oh Alice, just wait till you see what I got for us today." Brandon's lilting Irish voice was one of the reasons Alice had fallen in love with him all those years ago. Even with the monster he had become, his voice seemed to sprinkle over her like fairy dust – the fairy dust her sister Julia had thrown over her when they were kids, playing princess and fairy games.

Her face contorted, a tortured look taking over as she recalled her beautiful sister. Even she had succumbed to his charm, and when she had insisted on a visit, Alice had tried so hard to stop her from coming. She shook her head to stop those horrific memories from resurfacing.

Overhead the light flickered, and, in the distance, thunder rumbled like a horde of a thousand horsemen. A storm was coming, she thought, a storm was undeniably on its way. She struggled to wipe a tear from her eye as she went around to the rear of the car, following dutifully behind her tall, dark-haired husband. His good looks, lilting voice and placid demeanour were all working for him as he repeatedly went looking for new prey to feed his terrible addiction.

Her mind wandered to a time when she thought she could entice him to stop, to when she had participated in, even instigated, several episodes of sexually deviant behaviour to take his mind from the depraved thoughts he seemed plagued by. However, it seemed nothing she could do would ever be enough. Sure, it had slowed his need for a little while, to prey, abduct, rape and kill his victims, but it hadn't seemed to 'cure' him of his evil thoughts and behaviour.

She turned to help Brandon remove the large burlap sack from the back of the covered pickup. *God dammit*, she thought, *there are two heavy sacks this time. When will it end* she asked herself, *when will this nightmare end?*

She struggled with the weight of one of the sacks, down the two flights of stairs to the basement. Counting the steps in her head had become a ritual. Sixteen steps down, sixteen steps up. She stumbled slightly at the last step.

"Careful, you klutz. You have precious cargo there." His voice came booming down from the top of the stairs.

"Sorry," she called to him. "I'm so, so, sorry," she whispered to the sack.

Gently placing her load on the floor, she untied the rope and let the thick material fall to the sides. She gasped. There, curled up in a ball was the little boy, Kevin, from the next block up. Alice often took in sewing and Flora, Kevin's mum, was a customer of hers. She had some sheets she was repairing for her upstairs in her sewing basket. Alice had often seen Kevin riding his bike past her house after school.

She knelt down next to the boy. He was a gangly looking lad, only about thirteen or fourteen, she thought. She brushed the hair from his eyes gently. "Oh honey, I'm so sorry," she said as she picked the lad up in her arms, a dead weight in his drugged state, and carried him to the cot in the corner. She laid him on the bed and covered him with a travel blanket, returning to pick up the sack and putting it on the pile on the shelves on one wall.

"Aren't they marvellous?" Brandon asked her as he came down the stairs. "I've got the matching one right here."

He put the sack he was carrying down on the floor with a thump. Alice grimaced. She carefully undid the rope and gently removed the material from around Penny, Kevin's twin sister. The girl was drugged but murmuring. Brandon went over to the water jug and poured a glass of water for the girl, mixing a spoonful of powder into it from the special jar he kept locked in his tool cabinet. He pressed it to her lips and squeezed her cheeks to make her swallow it.

"I'm going up stairs to take a shower and watch the news. Is my dinner ready? Make sure they are all prepared for me about 8 o'clock Allie."

"Your dinner is in the oven, it's hot, so be careful when you take it out. They will be ready." Brandon kissed the top of his wife's head and disappeared up the basement stairs.

She busied herself taking Penny to the other cot and folding up the sack. She had a routine now. Undressing them quickly, then came the wash, followed by redressing in clean underwear that she kept on hand in a variety of sizes.

She would brush their hair and teeth then secure the chains, leaving a bottle of water within reach. This would usually take about an hour, or an hour and half if there were two of them. Alice would collect their clothes and shoes in a paper bag and dispose of them in the furnace later. Mostly they wouldn't have anything else on them, especially the homeless ones, but they would usually take a little longer to clean up. If they had items that would burn, like handkerchiefs or material handbags, they went into the furnace. Other items, like jewellery or mobile phones, she would put in a shoebox with some rocks, and leave them in the boot of the car for Brandon to throw into the river or the lake next time he went out.

She tried to switch her mind off while she worked. It was difficult, but she took special care of them, treating them nicely and gently and with respect, whoever they were. She could never justify what he did or even her part in it, but she just did not have the strength to do anything about it. Twice she had attempted to.

The first time she had tried to run away, getting as far as the highway before he caught her. The scars across her back a constant reminder of the beatings she endured the following weeks. The second time she had found his phone and tried to ring for help. She had hidden in the laundry closet and dialled but he had found her. Sometimes she wondered if he had left the phone for her to find, as though it were a test. She had no hearing in her left ear from the beatings from *that* attempt.

Crying out for help was out of the question. She didn't want to die in the furnace like the others. She had finished with Kevin and Penny now and had tidied up. She left the light on for them and the radio playing soft background music to calm them and went upstairs.

"All done? You're a good girl Allie. You know your place and do your job, that's why I love you sweetheart," Brandon complimented her. He had finished his dinner and was dressed in the ridiculous smoking jacket he liked to wear on these special evenings. He said it made him feel like the 'Lord of the Manor'.

"Yes Brandon. All done. I'll get on with the dishes and then some sewing I think."

"Ok," he gave her a peck on the cheek before heading off to the basement, "I'll sleep downstairs tonight, see you in the morning."

Alice didn't take long to clean up the kitchen and set up her sewing machine on the table. She had taken up sewing because it calmed her. The noise from the machine drowning out anything she might hear from the basement, was a bonus.

At first, she had only done sewing for the two of them.

Curtains, shirts, pants. Of course, there were also the burlap sacks. Then she had convinced Brandon that the extra money from sewing for others would come in handy and would go a long way towards showing the neighbours that they were a 'normal' couple.

When they had first moved here he had made sure they knew about his wife having a terrible case of agoraphobia and anthropophobia, so no nosey neighbours ever expected to see her out and about, nor would they come to visit.

A couple of years ago she had asked Brandon to put up a sign at the local market, so she could take in sewing and do alterations. People would call the number and leave a message on the answering machine. The phone was locked away, of course, but she had access to the answering machine. That's how he would communicate with her during the day, when he was out either at the office, or hunting his prey.

Brandon would call the customers back when he got home from work and arrange to pick up the items when he was out paying his weekly visit to the store on Saturday mornings. He would drop the items back to customers the following week. He'd supervise her preparing the repaired items, watching her wrap them with brown paper, so she could not use these packages to slip in a note, or anything he wouldn't approve of. Alice didn't charge much, for her it wasn't about the money. The sewing fulfilled a need, she needed to feel that she was still a valuable member of society, that she could contribute something useful.

As she was hemming Flora's new sheet and listening to a song on the radio, *Message in a Bottle,* her mind wandered as it often did. She would dream up scenarios where someone would come and rescue her, or there would be a bushfire and firemen would tear down the door to get in and discover her home prison. She had even semi-planned to start a fire in the house once but having seen the bodies burning in the furnace so many times she was terrified of dying by fire.

The lyrics of this song were hitting home; how it spoke of a lonely castaway on an island, wanting to be rescued; how this castaway used a bottle to send his S.O.S. to the world. Alice stopped sewing. She had unexpectedly had a thought. What if *she* could send an S.O.S to the world? What if she could sew her S.O.S to the world into a sheet? She picked up the second sheet from the other end of the kitchen table and unfolded it on to the spotlessly clean kitchen floor.

She had considered sending out notes of distress wrapped in the sewing a few times, but as Brandon always supervised her folding the garments and wrapping them there had never seemed to be a way she could use this means to get help.

The sheet had a 'right side' and a 'wrong side', she knew that. She also knew that housewives would generally put the top sheet on the bed upside down, so that when you folded back the edge on top of the blanket or doona, it had the right side showing, with no hem. She reasoned that if she used the edge of that right side to sew a message - an S.O.S message – then, when Flora put the sheet on the bed and folded back the edge, she would be able to read it. By Saturday the twins would have been missing for four days, so Flora would be in the right state of mind to take the message seriously. She and her husband would be distraught by then.

Alice knew she still had another couple of hours before Brandon would appear, so she quickly rethreaded her machine with a pale cream thread. She wanted the message to be read but it was important that Brandon could not see it while he watched her fold the sheets and wrap them. She couldn't use a bright red cotton or anything obvious, however, being a woman, she knew that when Flora made the bed she would either notice the cream thread against the white sheet, or, while smoothing the folded edge on the blanket she would feel the raised letters.

She took a few minutes to decide what to write, then set her machine up for embroidering letters. It didn't take long; less than twenty minutes and she was done. She finished the rest of the hemming on both sheets and folded them loosely on top of the sewing box.

She would fold them and wrap them on Saturday morning under Brandon's supervision, then he could deliver them. Alice smiled inwardly at the irony of Brandon delivering her *Message in a Bottle* or in this case her *Message in a Sheet*.

The next three days seemed to pass in a blur. All Alice could think about were the sheets. She helped Brandon clean up each day, went about her normal household duties and scrubbed the basement, bringing food to the drugged children twice a day. By Saturday morning she began to be concerned that he would tire of Kevin and Penny and that he might well want to dispose of them before Flora would get her message.

"Right, I have the shopping list Allie, do you want to wrap this sewing please and I can drop it off on the way to the store." Brandon picked up the brown paper and string from

100

the top shelf of the pantry cupboard.

"Ok. I'll just get the sheets." She picked up the loosely folded sheets from the top of the sewing basket under the side table in the kitchen. She laid out the paper and shook the top sheet out in front of Brandon. Her heart was beating so loudly she wondered if he would hear it. She folded the sheet in half and then in quarters. She continued until it was approximately the size of an A4 piece of paper, then put it on top of the brown paper. She did the same for the bottom sheet, then placed that on top.

"Hold it!" Brandon called out loudly from the other end of the table. Alice froze on the spot. She could barely breathe.

"You missed something. There's a bit of thread hanging from the corner." Brandon reached into the sewing box and extracted the pinking shears. He carefully snipped a cream piece of cotton, hanging from the edge of the sheet, and returned the shears to the basket. Alice breathed again and quickly wrapped the brown paper package and tied the string.

"See you Allie. Won't be long. Can we have that tuna casserole for dinner tonight, honey?" Brandon kissed his wife and left.

Alice flopped down into the reading chair by the window and breathed a sigh of relief. So far, so good. Now to wait. She anticipated that Flora would open the parcel when she got it, and with any luck she would want to put the sheets on the bed today, or perhaps tomorrow – a lot of folks changed their linen on the weekends - she hoped Flora was one of them! She decided she would busy herself with making dinner, and she meant to get on and give the refrigerator a good clean today too. It was after four o'clock when Brandon returned. He was in a grumpy mood, so she went to the garage and helped to bring in the shopping. "Did you drop off the sheets?" she asked casually.

"Yeah, her husband was there. He paid, the money is in the envelope on the front seat. I'm going into the den to read, then watch the game. Dinner at six?"

"Sure. I made the casserole you like." She finished taking the shopping inside, packed it away, and started on the fridge.

Another three days passed slowly. She busied herself with housework and she had two new sewing jobs to start. By the end of the third day she was sure Flora would see the message, but alas, no one came, no one called.

By the end of the second week after she had sewn the S.O.S. into the sheet, she had given up hope. Maybe using the cream thread had not been such a good idea after all.

Brandon had disposed of Kevin and Penny last Tuesday. Alice had spent the afternoon in her room, saying prayers for them. By Friday she recognised that hungry look in his eyes. She was not sure she could go on any more. She had considered trying to end her life many times, but she truly didn't think she was brave enough. Besides, something inside her always said that if she did that, he would win. He would have beaten her down and she could not face that.

Friday evening, he went out, and she stood by the window and watched the world go by outside. At dusk she sat in her reading chair and must have dozed a little, because suddenly she heard an almighty crash and two policemen with a battering ram came flying through the front door.

"Oh my God," she cried out, startled and afraid.

"Everyone get down on the floor, NOW!" The two detectives behind the policemen were flashing their badges and yelling into the house. People seemed to be running all over the place.

Alice knelt on the floor then lay face down on the rug with her hands above her head. "It's ok,' she answered timidly, "I'm the only one here. He's out. Brandon's out in the pickup."

"Okay ma'am. You can get up now. Sit right there, in the chair. My name is Detective O'Reilly, and this is Constable Learmonth. Are you Alice? Alice Vickers? Is there anyone else at all in the house right now?" The burly detective put away his badge and gun and sat on the couch opposite Alice.

"No sir. Just me. I am Alice Vickers. Brandon's out right now. He should be back soon though. He won't like it if you are in his house."

"That's alright ma'am, we have a warrant for your husband's arrest, and a search warrant for your house. Now, let me ask you, did you sew a message on Flora Ponting's sheet? Were you asking for help?" the Detective's voice had softened, it was soothing and deep.

"Yes sir. I most certainly did. I didn't think Mrs Ponting had seen it as she never came around or called me or anything." Alice answered, flustered and a little short of breath.

"Oh yes, Alice, she most certainly did see it. She contacted us yesterday and we have had your husband and your house under surveillance all day today. She didn't see it right away as she was distraught about her children going missing of course, and didn't change the linen that week, or in fact, undertake any housework, as you can imagine." The detective explained, "However, when her sister came to stay and unwrapped the new sheets for the spare room, she noticed the unusual stitching along the folded edge and asked Mrs Ponting about it. They thought it might be a cryptic message for ransom, so they came straight to us about it. Alice. May I call you Alice?"

"Certainly," Alice replied.

"Well Alice, we need you to tell us now where the children are and what's been happening here in your home."

He had a calming manner about him, making Alice feel relaxed and safe for the first time in many years. "Just tell us simply, in your own words. Start anywhere you like."

"Ok. How about I start at the beginning. Twenty-two years ago, Brandon and I got married. A year after that it started…" Alice sighed, and as she began her terrible tale tears streamed down her cheeks.

* * *

Brandon showed up two hours later. The police had moved all their cars and had the street under surveillance, so they knew when he arrived. They waited until he drove into the garage and then they pounced.

He had been carted off in a van, not even bothering to ask after Alice. It would not have mattered. She had been taken to a new location, a part of a special section of the witness protection program that dealt with domestic abuse victims.

The house at 37 Tristan Way had been completely sealed off, as a crime scene. It would take a full four months to process the house, particularly the furnace and they would end up uncovering the DNA of more than twenty individuals. Nine other premises across four states were also put into lockdown.

The papers would later report the details of Brandon Vickers, his twenty-one years of serial killing, and journalists would label him with a very appropriate nickname. Mostly, they treated his wife kindly, as they pointed out repeatedly she too was a victim, of this insane man. Alice spent the rest of her life in an assisted living facility in a state far away from where her husband was incarcerated. She knew she was lucky to still be alive, but still she suffered every day…living with the knowledge that she had been married to *the burlap sack cremator*.

The Removal

"Number 35, that's it Bob, the next driveway on the left, mate. Just pull up out front, we can manoeuvre the truck later, although it looks pretty good to load from there. It's a short driveway. What do ya reckon?" Harry asked his offsider, who was driving the large removal truck.

"Yeah mate, if I park halfway up on the verge we should be able to walk straight down the drive, up the ramp and into the back I reckon," Bob replied, pulling the vehicle over with two wheels up on the nature strip between the footpath and the road.

After gathering the paperwork and attaching it to his clipboard Harry hurried up to the front door to meet Mr and Mrs Harrison, the clients. Bob did his usual, went to the back of the truck, opened the doors, set up the ramps, unhooked the trolleys and prepared the blankets ready for wrapping around the most precious furniture.

Bob and Harry had been partners in their small, local removal business now for over twelve years. Like an old married couple, they'd settled into a comfortable relationship, having got to know each other's quirks and limits.

Harry always took care of the paperwork. Bob had not fared well at school and was probably a little slow when it came to understanding forms, and although he'd never say it to his face, Harry thought his partner's handwriting left a lot to be desired. The last time Harry had let Bob fill in an inventory sheet he'd had a terrible time trying to decipher the entries at the delivery end of the removal, so it was certainly better if he looked after that side of things himself.

Bob had some good skills though. They'd worked hard to start their own business together and now it had reached a stage where the men could pretty much pick and choose their jobs. Cutting back to working only five days a week from the original seven suited them both, giving them a lot more family time, which they valued.

Bob had always been a strong man. He had worked on the railroad for many years. His perseverance and 'never say die' attitude was something that Harry greatly admired. There wasn't any piece of furniture too heavy, too big or too awkward for the removalist. He would think about it, rethink it, and nine times out of ten the man would get it packed into the truck perfectly. Each piece would take up the least amount of room possible and Bob would make certain that everything was stacked and well secured. This had resulted in them building a great reputation over the years. They were renowned for achieving on-time removals, at a reasonable cost, with no damages, scratches, dents or breakages.

"Morning Mrs Harrison, nice to see you again. I hope you're all ready for the big move," Harry smiled as he greeted the woman who came to answer the door. Harry's forte, along with being the 'brains' of the operation, was his people skills.

He was great with everyone. He got on well with kids, the old dears simply loved him (he did tend to use his flirtatious skills on everyone, so that probably helped) and most people found him very easy to talk to. He tended to use his listening skills so well that you thought you were the only person in the world who mattered to him at that moment in time.

It worked a treat in this business, where you needed to build a rapport with people at the first meeting and instil in clients a feeling of trust. After all, you were going to be responsible for taking all their material goods, possessions they had worked hard for, perhaps everything they owned in this world, to a new location. Sometimes it was just a few streets away, other times the move might be across the country. Either way you needed the client to believe in you, to be confident that you would care for their belongings as if they were your own. Harry was good at that.

"Come in Harry, we're all ready. Please, call me Jackie," Mrs Harrison gave a little giggle, opened the door for him and stepped back into the hallway, "Where do you want to start?"

Harry moved past her and straight into the front room. Another of Harry's helpful skills was his terrific memory. He could remember the layout of a house, the items of furniture and possessions in each room, and was able to estimate the amount of removal boxes each would require after just one walk-a-round. Today's job would start in the living room and move through the dining, kitchen and laundry. They would take heavy furniture items and white goods from each room, then move back to the bedrooms for the beds, cupboards and chests of drawers. Each room had numerous big pieces of furniture, but not a lot of little, incidental items, which was a good thing.

After the furniture they would take the boxes, which Harry noted were packed and placed along one wall in each room, as he had instructed the Harrison's last week on their walk-a-round visit. This should be a quick, easy job, he thought. They would be well and truly finished by two o'clock, which meant he could give Bob an early mark, so he could go home to his wife Karen, and the kids. Bob still had young ones at home, his boy about nine years old and the girl nearly thirteen.

Harry didn't think very highly of Karen. She didn't work or appear to do much. He thought she was pleasant enough, but sometimes tended to come across a bit 'holier than thou'. Harry, a down to earth man, didn't appreciate people with airs and graces, but he was always polite to her as Bob was a treasured friend and business partner.

Harry's tribe had finally left home last year, the youngest, Dylan, enlisting in the army and the other three were away at University. Two of his kids lived over east, one was studying art and the other a specialist law degree.

Harry's daughter, Matilda, lived up near her local campus in the city, just fifty kilometres from Harry and his wife Pearl. He had adjusted well to the kids finally moving out and getting on with their lives, but Pearl was still having some issues becoming an 'empty nester' as the media often termed it. She had spent the greater part of her life looking after the children, occasionally working, when they needed it, but always putting the kids first. Now that she didn't have the day-to-day demands of a family she was finding it hard to know which direction to choose for the next stage in her life. She'd taken on some volunteer work a few weeks ago, so hopefully that would help.

"So, Graham and I thought we would just pop out for a quick, umm, coffee, with our neighbours Sue and Will if that's alright with you," Jackie was explaining to him.

"We thought you probably wouldn't want us to be right on top of you while you work," she continued with a wink, "We'll be back before lunch though."

Jackie broke Harry's train of thought and brought him back into the room and to the job at hand.

"Of course, Jackie. What a good idea. You and Graham deserve that after all the hard work you've done getting everything ready for us. Terrific job I must say! It certainly makes our job easier if we have great prep work like you guys have done. Thanks for that!"

Bob just caught the tail end of the conversation as he joined them in the living room and added, "Sure does. This looks marvellous Mrs Harrison. I'm going to get started right here Harry, ok?"

"Yup," Harry replied, "Let's get his show on the road. Take your time Jackie."

With that Harry and Bob threw themselves into taking load after load of furniture out to the van while the Harrisons made themselves scarce for the morning. The men found that many clients preferred to do that, rather than get in the way as they traipsed back and forth to the removal truck.

Of course, there was the other type of client too. The sort

that wanted to stand and 'direct' you, as though they knew more about the business than you did.

Mostly the men managed to weed those kinds of clients out now. They had become adept at spotting them during the initial interview and walk-a-round and if either of the men had qualms about a new client they openly discussed it when they returned to the office.

It was a lot easier to tell someone on the phone that they were very sorry 'but the dates they requested were just not available', than to have one of those clients standing over them every moment of the job.

Those ones tended to be a problem at the delivery end too, requiring pieces of furniture to be moved from room to room, then back to where they started, as they changed their minds again and again. It was often difficult to tell them nicely that although they had paid for a removal, this did not include a home decorating service with a couple of labourers at their disposal for an entire day.

Having worked solidly for nearly three hours, Harry started feeling hungry so went to find Bob. He was out at the truck, tying in the final piece of furniture before they started loading the boxes. This next part always went quickly as the boxes were all standard sizes, the truck fitting three high and four wide. With each of them bringing out two boxes at a time on the dolly's they would only be around for another hour and a half to two hours, then they would be done.

"Lunch break Bob," Harry called to his partner, "Come and get it buddy."

"Be right there Harry. Do you want to sit out the back,

under that patio? I noticed that there's two fold-up chairs out there," Bob's voice filtered out from the back of the truck.

Harry carried the esky and Bob grabbed his phone from the cab. They made their way through the house and flopped down in the folding chairs, under the shady patio. Bob sent a quick text to Karen, letting her know they should be finished early and then unwrapped his lunch.

Harry opened the esky and removed his carefully prepared sandwiches, a container with two pieces of fried chicken and a generous slab of home-made lemon cake with coconut icing.

It wasn't so bad that Pearl had lots of time on her hands now. Last year he could remember being just like Bob, slapping together a vegemite sandwich and a piece of fruit and a couple of store-bought biscuits most days, as his wife was busy ferrying kids to school or participating on school committees. Things had certainly improved in the kitchen since Dylan left home. Pearl would spend her time baking, frying chicken, whizzing up home-made casseroles and frittatas.

Harry bit into a healthy tuna and salad sandwich. "What ya got today fella?" he asked his mate.

"Had to make my own this morning. Karen had her hands full. I slapped together peanut butter sandwiches and a couple of Tim Tams – a special treat because we had the in-laws for dinner last night."

"Well, I've got an extra piece of fried chicken and a huge slab of lemon cake if you're interested? No way I can eat all this lot. Pearl is forever sending too much food," Harry replied, leaning over to pass Bob the chicken and cake.

"Thanks heaps, appreciate it boss. That cake looks delicious!" Bob grabbed the food gratefully, taking a huge bite of the chicken straight away.

The men spent the next ten minutes sitting in companionable silence, munching their lunch. Bob got a few texts, probably replies or instructions from Karen, then both put away their rubbish and returned to get the rest of the job done. "I'll start in the front and you work from the back if you like mate," said Harry, indicating the living room. He put the inventory sheet in the kitchen and wheeled his dolly into the lounge room.

Bob picked up his dolly and headed off down the hallway to the home office located at the back.

The first load went off without a hitch and Bob returned for the second while Harry continued at the front of the house. Things were going along swimmingly, until Bob's phone buzzed again and just for a moment he lost his concentration and took the corner of the hall a little too wide. He could see he was going to clip the edge of the second bedroom doorway so came to a sudden halt to make sure he didn't do any damage to the wall. Stumbling backwards he wavered ever so slightly and lost control of the dolly. Bob went down, the dolly swung forward, then back, then landed right on top of him.

"Oh, thank God for that," he exclaimed, laying backwards on the floor of the hallway, the dolly and two packing boxes on top of him, "no damage done!" He edged the boxes off himself and stood up slowly.

Bending over and righting the dolly, he then proceeded to stack the two boxes right way up again. Bob noticed that the tape had come off the bottom of one of those boxes. He turned it sideways and as he did the bottom burst open, tossing some books, a pillow and a wooden trinket box on to the carpet.

"Damn," he muttered as he hastened to pick up the items. After stacking them up he went to get the spare roll of tape from the kitchen.

Returning to the pile he taped up the bottom of the box and then lifted the items, returning them carefully to the top of the box. As he did so an envelope, a key ring and a little plastic-coated book slipped out of the trinket box. That's when Bob realised he had the wooden box upside down.

It had come out of the packing box and tumbled, falling on to the carpet. Feeling a little embarrassed he picked up the bits and pieces and went to put them back into the wooden trinket box. The envelope and key ring fitted easily but he had trouble getting the little plastic book into the box. It appeared to be one of those 'brag books' that people put pictures of their grand kids in, and as he tried to gently ease it back into the box it flicked open and one of the pictures fell out.

"Good grief!" Bob exclaimed. "It never rains but it pours." He bent over and grabbed the picture, preparing to stuff it back into the photo album.

Bob gasped.

He took a second look, bringing the picture closer to focus more clearly on the image. He looked sheepishly around, but he was still alone. "Oh, my Lord above," Bob shook his head, unable to fully comprehend what was before his eyes.

He turned the photo over a couple of times and blinked rapidly. It was taking a while for the disturbing image to settle into his brain. Bob was holding in his hand a full colour photo of two people, a man and a woman, completely naked and intimately involved in some sort of sexual act. Not only that, but the part that was blowing his mind was that the woman was Pearl. Harry's wife! And the man was Mr Harrison, their current client.

Quickly, as though he could 'un-see' it, Bob shoved the picture back into the little photo album, bending it slightly in his haste. He stole another nervous look down the hallway and placed the album back into the wooden box, securing the lid and shoving the box into the removal carton.

He was just about to tape the top of the box up when he hesitated. He really wasn't sure what to do. His loyalty and friendship with his best mate Harry had him confused. Did he hide this terrible fact from his friend? He hated the idea of telling Harry his wife was unfaithful. Or, did he show him the picture, knowing that if it were his own wife he would certainly want to know. He taped the top but continued to stand there, totally perplexed.

"Hey, mate. You taking a break or something? I've finished the front rooms; do you want me to start in the last bedroom?" Harry startled Bob as he came down the hallway.

"Umm, yeah, I just had a bit of a spill, but I've sorted it now Harry," Bob answered, trying to sound casual. "I only have four more boxes in that far room then we are done."

"Ok," his partner turned as if to continue down the hallway. He turned back and looked at Bob, cocking his head to one side. "Hey, are you alright buddy? You look like you've seen a ghost. I'll finish these if you like, why don't you take a five-minute break. Go get a bottle of cold water and sit on the chair in the shade." Harry looked concerned now.

"I'm ok boss. It's just … It's just that … Actually, I'm not sure how to put this," the man stuttered. Bob was lost for words, certainly not sure he was doing the right thing, but he just couldn't bring himself to cover up what he had found.

"You'd better take a gander at this mate," he said, leaning over and ripping the tape off the top of the carton. Retrieving the wooden box, he placed the photo album into Harry's hands. Opening the first page the loose photo was right there for his friend to see.

Bob looked away. He didn't want Harry to see him looking at a picture of Pearl, especially not a naked picture. He didn't want to make him feel even more ashamed. Bob moved a step or two down the hallway, to give Harry some privacy so he could take it all in. Behind him he heard a guttural sound, and for a moment he though Harry had started crying.

"Oh my God! Seriously!" Harry exclaimed. Then he burst out laughing. "God dammit Bob, you should see the look on your face! Mate, you've gone white as a sheet. I think you'd better sit down buddy."

Harry took Bob's elbow and steered him up the hallway to the kitchen and out the sliding door to the patio. He guided his friend to the fold-up chairs and waited till Bob had seated himself in one.

"Good grief mate. That must have given you a hell of a shock. Seeing my Pearl, in all her glory. Stark naked and all."

He handed Bob a bottle of water from the esky that still sat by the chair from their lunch break. "Sorry, I never meant for you to find out like this. I should have told you before, I just couldn't bring myself to find the right time. It's like this, you and Karen have quite a different relationship to me and my Pearl. We've had a, what you might call, 'different' type of marriage for the past twenty years." Harry went on, while Bob sat with his mouth open.

He was hardly able to comprehend what his friend was telling him. "We have always been swingers you see. We love each other to bits, but we get our fun and keep our marriage alive by participating in swingers' parties," Harry continued, "Mostly we go to them, very occasionally we host one, but that hasn't happened often because of the kids."

His mate leaned over and patted Bob's shoulder, "We could only ever do that when they were all away at camp, or that year you guys took them all fishing for that long weekend."

Harry pulled up the other fold-up chair next to his partner and patted his knee reassuringly as he talked. "We didn't tell you and Karen because we didn't want it to make our friendship awkward. You are good, God-fearing folk, Bob, and we know how you both feel about marriage. We were pretty sure you would disapprove of our life-style choice, so we just kept it to ourselves. We didn't want to let it interfere with our friendship with you and Karen."

Harry breathed deeply then let out a sigh. "I guess we should have given you a heads-up before now, but it's just a hell of a co-incidence that you found that photo, and if you

117

hadn't, you would never have known." Harry looked at Bob and said sincerely, "Mate, I hope this doesn't change anything between us. You know I regard you as my best friend and I love you like a brother. I'd hate to lose that."

The removalist turned towards his friend, "No, of course you won't. But it sure would have been better if you'd given me the heads-up. It was one hell of a shock finding that picture, and then not knowing what to do about it!"

Bob put out his hand for his mate to shake. "It certainly doesn't matter to me what you guys do in your private lives. Let's get this job finished shall we, so we can head home to our women."

Harry shook his business partner's hand and they finished up the removal. Bob waited in the truck while Mrs Harrison signed off on the paperwork and after they returned to the depot he said goodnight and waved to his boss as he headed off home.

The next morning when Harry arrived for work he found an envelope under the front door to the office. Harry ripped it open and read Bob's resignation. It saddened him. For the first time in his life he began to seriously regret some of the choices he'd made. He never saw his best mate again.

Captive Princess

Looking longingly through the window, she watched the rain fall softly on the street below. Although she was being held captive, she always treasured these moments, when she was alone in the house. The doors to the upstairs loft apartment in the old warehouse were firmly locked and dead-bolted from the outside and the iron bars on the windows completed her 'prison cell'. But on days like today, especially in this little room with the big window, she felt like she was a princess.

Gazing out the window of her castle turret at her kingdom below, she knew every inch of the street, the buildings and the landscape intimately, although she had never walked around them. She knew and cared about *her people* – those who lived and worked in this block, as though they were her closest friends or relatives, even though they had never met.

Her observational powers were exceptional, and her imagination was honed now, much more so than when she had first arrived, over fifteen years ago. She had been only nine then, and after the initial months spent crying, begging, pleading, cajoling, bargaining and screaming for her freedom, she had eventually resigned herself to the fact that no-one was coming to rescue her and that she could not escape.

She had spent a long time exploring her prison cell, including the floor-to-ceiling bookshelves. Over time she had read each one of the ninety-two books shelved there, from cover to cover, she had learned to accept her reality and to only retreat to her fantasy land when the beast was away. There she was the princess, to be rescued by a handsome prince on a white horse. He would be tall, handsome and wear a suit of armour that shone in the sunlight. She would sit here alone, re-reading a book, sewing, mending or darning socks, and visualise him arriving, taking her up on his horse and they would ride off together.

He would whisk her off, to a land far away, where they would marry, and he could care for her and treat her like a princess. Brushing her hair lovingly, taking her face in his hands, he would kiss her lips, her cheeks, her eyelids and whisper tenderly, over and over, just how much he loved her.

A teardrop slowly made its way down her cheek to her lip – it tasted salty she thought, like rain from the sea – if you could even get rain on the sea. She tried hard to remember the sea. Her parents had taken her there once. They had driven for hours and she remembered being cooped up with her annoying little brother in the back seat of the old station wagon playing 'I spy with my little eye' or travel bingo. She remembered her little brother fondly now, not really being able to see his face any more, as it would have changed so much. He would be all grown up, a handsome young man of about twenty years old. When was his birthday? It must have been in January because it would come around not long after Christmas. She could recall how she used to get upset because he got more presents the week after Christmas and she would miss out.

Thud. Clunk. Slide.

The noises broke into her reverie and she got up quickly from the window and went to check on the stew she had simmering on the stove. "Hi honey, I'm home." His sing song voice was painful to her ears, like a cheese grater on skin. He snickered to himself. "How's my little Princess today?"

She wondered what he would think if he knew about her fantasies, and how she spent her time imagining being a real princess. But no, she thought, he doesn't have the capacity to think that she would ever have fantasies.

He would not be able to comprehend that she might ever imagine being anywhere else but here, with him. "What's for dinner honey? I'm starving!"

"I've made you a beef stew, with garlic and herb dumplings, just as you like it," she replied.

He leaned into her then, trying to kiss her neck, but she turned away, as if she hadn't seen him coming and stirred the pot.

"I must go and set the table, why don't you wash up? Shall I switch on the television, so you can watch the news with your dinner?" she asked.

It had taken many years before she had finally been allowed to control the television. It had been locked in a secure cupboard until he was sure that she would not watch things he did not authorise. But now she mainly used it to control *him*. With the television on he would concentrate his attention on the screen instead of her, and if she could get him to polish off two or three beers early, he would fall asleep before 9 o'clock, which would be perfect.

"Oh, you do spoil me you know," he laughed, appreciating the irony that he found in the fact that she was forced to do this, she did not have a choice. She had been trained over the years, that, to have free reign over the loft and not be shackled or chained up each day, she must treat him respectfully, even lovingly, as though they were a normal, happily married couple. She returned to the kitchen to butter some bread and finish setting the table.

Hearing him close the door to the bathroom she grimaced, remembering that she had left a handtowel on the floor behind the door earlier. It had fallen from the rack, but having her hands full of dirty washing, she hadn't been able to pick it up. Damn, she hoped he wouldn't notice it.

Crash!

"Arrgghh," his voice came from the other room.

She was startled and nearly dropped the stew pot, the shout was so loud. Goodness me, he had only had one beer, what was he doing stumbling around in the bathroom already. It usually took him three or four beers to become that clumsy! She put the pot down, wiped her hands and went to see what all the fuss was about. The bathroom door was shut so she knocked gently, "Are you ok?" she asked timidly. There was no answer. She knocked again, a little louder this time. "Are you ok?"

Still no answer. She gently twisted the handle and pushed the door, but it would not budge. It wasn't locked, as it had opened just a fraction, but something was stopping it from opening right up. She put a bit of muscle to the door, wondering if the washing basket or the towel rack had fallen and was jamming the door shut. The door moved an inch. She wiggled herself into position, turning and leaning against the door, planting her feet on the floor and pushing with her thighs and back. The door inched open, very slowly.

She stopped for a minute to catch her breath, wondering why he wasn't answering her. Perhaps he was too angry to answer. She was sure it was going to be her fault if something had fallen over.

She steadied herself and gave the door one last shove. It opened another four or five inches, enough for her to be able to squeeze her head through the opening to sneak a look.

She squealed and pulled her head back out of the door frame. Her hands flew to her mouth. She couldn't fully comprehend what she had just seen, but it looked as though he had slipped on the hand-towel behind the door, fallen, hit his head on the bath tub and there was blood everywhere. He appeared to be bleeding from a cut above the eye and from a gash on the back of his head. He was laying on his back, glassy eyes staring up to the ceiling. It was his body weight that had jammed the door shut.

She paused for a deep breath and risked another look. Yes, he had unquestionably tripped on the hand-towel. It was still lodged under one shoe. Stealing another look at his face she wasn't quite sure if he was still alive, his eyes had glazed over, and he wasn't moving. She watched his chest. There was a tiny rise and fall.

Backing away from the door towards the lounge, she felt confused. Perching on the edge of the sofa, she took a few more deep breaths to clear her head.

After a few minutes she decided to take one more peak at him. She was loath to phone an ambulance, but how could she get away with not calling them? She poked her head around the door and watched the blood continue to trickle from the back of his head, along with his laboured, shallow breathing, for another couple of minutes.

Then, without touching anything else, she leaned over and grabbed the hand-towel, taking it back into the kitchen, wrapping it in a plastic shopping bag and stuffing it deep into the rubbish bin, under the vegetable scraps. She carried her bowl of stew, with a piece of bread, to the table, and calmly ate her meal. The food seemed to revive her. Her thinking became clearer.

Fifteen minutes later she had finished her meal. She busied herself tidying up her bowl and plate and setting his meal on the table for him. She went to the fridge and removed three bottles of beer, emptying the first two down the sink and placing the empty bottles strategically on the living room floor, where they usually finished up at the end of the night. She took the other bottle to the bathroom. His breathing had stopped now. She stood and watched for several minutes before emptying the third beer over him and the floor and dropping the glass bottle to the tile floor, where it shattered. The amber liquid weaved its way through the blood, mixing with it and winding its way to the drain in the centre of the tiled floor.

Returning to the living room and picking up her knitting, she wandered over to her armchair and turned on the television. She flicked to a channel which had a cooking show she enjoyed and settled in to watch. Thirty minutes later, as the show finished, she searched for his mobile phone in his work jacket, and then she dialled.

"Help, can you help me please? My husband has fallen in the bathroom and he won't get up. I'm very worried, there is lots of blood. Please help. Send an ambulance, please," she managed to infuse her voice with what she imagined to be just the right balance of fright and concern.

"Ok miss, just calm down. Take a deep breath. What's your address there?"

The operator had a lovely voice, she thought. It had been a long time since she had made contact with the outside world, but she knew it wouldn't be appropriate for her to just sit and chat. "Umm, I don't know the street address here, I'm really sorry. Can't you trace this phone or something? The cross street I can see from my window is called Randolph Avenue. Is that any help? And we are just a few streets from the river, I can see that in the distance on a clear day."

"Ok, that's fine miss. We will locate you. Are you in any danger?"

"No, I'm fine, but I should get back to my husband and try to help him. I will put the phone down now, but tell the medics that we are upstairs, in the front of the building, and the door is locked. They will have to bust it down."

"What? What do you mean? Can't you unlock the door? From the inside. Are you saying you are locked in?" the operator began to sound anxious now.

"Yes, I am locked in. The door has a deadbolt on both sides, and the keys are in my husband's pocket. I can't get them out. I have to go now, please hurry."

She disconnected and put the phone down on the table.

Hurrying back into the bathroom she spent a few minutes going through the motions of kneeling next to him, bending over him, ripping his shirt open and pushing on his chest a couple of times. Mostly it was to make sure she had just the right amount of blood on her, and the marks on the floor would be consistent with her story.

She loved to watch the police shows on the television when he was away each day. CSI was her favourite. She thought she had a pretty good idea how to 'stage' an attempted rescue scene.

She held her head in her hands and wiped her brow, then stood up to view herself in the mirror. "Perfect!" she exclaimed to her reflection. "You definitely look like someone who's tried to help her poor bleeding husband. It's a shame you didn't succeed though." She smiled a wry smile and returned to the living room.

Knock, knock, knock.

"Hello, anyone there? This is Constable Knight, from the Hampton Police and I have the paramedics here with me. We had a distress call to this address, are you there ma'am?" a deep voice boomed on the other side of the door. She edged closer to the voice.

"Yes, hello. I'm here," she cried out tentatively, "but I can't unlock the door. It's bolted on the inside. You will have to break it down."

"Ok ma'am. Please step right away from the door, we don't want you to get injured," the voice replied.

Thud. Thud. Thud.

Three loud thumps rung out on the other side of the door.

"Stay back ma'am. We are going to give it another go."

Thud. Thud. Thud.

Thud. Thud. Thud.

The timber around the metal hinges on the door-jam finally splintered. The door fell inwards, swinging back to front as it pivoted on the deadbolt instead of its hinges.

He stepped through the door and caught her, just as she fainted.

As she regained consciousness she realised she was in his arms. His big, thick, muscular arms were around her, cradling her like a baby. He had apparently brought her downstairs and they were exiting the front door of the warehouse into the street. The first thing she noticed was a big, white, police horse, tied up to a street lamp. Tears welled up and then flooded down her cheeks. "H-horse," she whispered to the man dressed in a blue police uniform, with sparkling brass buttons down the front of his shirt and shiny metal on his epaulets, who was holding her tightly.

"Yes ma'am. I'm part of the new mounted police squad here in town, and I was patrolling the river bank when the call came in. I was first on the scene. You just rest now, we will have you in the ambulance in no time."

She let the tears flow, certain that they all thought she was crying for her poor, dead 'husband' upstairs, but she knew, in her heart, that they were tears of happiness. Finally, her dream had come true, and she had been rescued by her 'knight' in shining 'armour' and his great white steed.

Answering Machine

Peering through the blinds, he anxiously awaited the arrival of the police. Surely, they would be here soon. He had called them hours ago, hadn't he? Well, it certainly seemed like hours. It was probably at least twenty minutes ago anyway. He had taken the phone with him to the window, so he could keep an eye on the house while he spoke to 000.

* * *

Let's go back, to where it started.

It had been your typical Friday evening. Mathew had arrived home from work around 6pm, turned on the television and flicked over to a news station, poured himself a scotch with a little ice, and downed a nice big mouthful. Kicking his shoes off, he perched on the side of the lounge, looking at the screen while pushing the button on the answering machine that had been blinking furiously when he got home. He'd thought it was probably more of those telephone canvassing calls he often got. Sometimes you could get two or three in a day. Don't they realise people go to work? They aren't likely to call back when they get home either!

"Matt? Help me please! There's someone outside the door. I think they are trying to break in. Are you home Matt? Help me, please!"

Mathew stood up. *God*, he thought, *its Renee*. His neighbour, Renee Simpson, had moved in only a few weeks back and they had immediately struck up a friendship. He had offered his help any time she needed it, and he ended up moving a bed into her spare room for her. They had shared a coffee on the porch that day and had spoken every couple of days after.

They had even had a glass of wine together last Friday night, and he had considered asking her out on a proper 'date' but hadn't quite worked up the courage just yet. He recognised her voice immediately.

The machine stopped then, and after a few seconds moved on to the next message. It took a second for Mathew to realise that the next message was playing.

"Matt? Are you there? Please pick up! I don't know who else to call. There's someone trying to get into my house. I'm going to hide upstairs now, in the closet. Please help me!"

She sounds terrified, Matt thought, *I don't know what to do*. The beep came again, and the machine moved on to the next message.

"Matt, I'm hiding in the closet upstairs. I brought the phone up here with me. I think he's inside the house Matt. I can't remember if I shut the window. Oh my God. I think he's in the kitchen. Please Matt, help me, please!"

130

Matt got up and walked to the window. He looked across the street to number fifty-seven just as the machine progressed to the next message.

"Matt, please…" the terror in Renee's voice had escalated as she begged him over the phone for help. "Can you come Matt? Please! He's downstairs, I can hear him going through the cupboards. He's been in the kitchen and the dining room, now he's moved into the living room. Oh my God! I can hear him on the stairs now," she broke off with a sob.

From his window Matt could see her house clearly. There looked to be a bluish grey sedan with its lights on, parked in front of the house, up towards Mrs Spicer's little bungalow.

The Millar kids were playing in the front yard, two doors up from there, but otherwise the street looked bare and normal, as it did at dusk every evening.

That's one of the things Renee had mentioned that she loved about Oakleigh, and particularly Smyth Street. She appreciated, like he did, that it was a quiet, family-oriented neighbourhood. She had said she truly looked forward to settling down here. She hadn't said much about where she had come from, just that it was up north, near a big city. She'd been equally reticent about sharing information regarding her family or friends or any other details of her past.

He glanced up and down the street, not seeing anything out of the ordinary. At Renee's home it appeared as though there was a light on in the front room and one upstairs. He couldn't remember the layout exactly, but he thought that room to the right was the spare room, where they had moved the bed that day, so the light could be coming from her room on the left.

"Matt, are you there Matt?" Renee's voice was now a whisper. "I heard him come up the stairs. I think he went into the office, he rummaged in there and now he's in the spare room. I don't know what to do. I'm in the closet in my bedroom, hiding under a blanket behind the evening gowns but if he comes in here he's sure to see me... help me Matt, pleeeease," she begged.

The answering machine shut itself off and rewound.

Matt was distraught. Still no sign of any assistance from the police. No-one appeared to be coming. He looked around his home. He didn't have a weapon of any sort. He wasn't too sure what he could do on his own. Maybe he could make a whole lot of noise, as though he was her husband coming home, or something. That might scare the guy off. He sprang into action, heading upstairs to the spare room where he had his old baseball bat in the cupboard. It's the only thing he could think of to arm himself with. He turned the lights on in the living room. The television was on already, so from the street it would still appear as though he was inside, watching the news.

He made his way to the rear of the house, through the kitchen and out into the backyard. If he went out the back gate he should be able to creep down the alley that ran parallel to the street then at the end of the alley he could turn on to the side street, creep across to the alley behind Renee's, and enter through her back gate.

He grabbed his black hoodie from the coat rack as he went out the door and put it on over his business shirt.

Gently he closed the back door and went carefully, quietly,

but quickly to the alley. As usual there was only Mr Simpson's van in the alley, so he crept around that and headed to the side street.

Once there it was easy to keep in the shadows and cross Smyth Street, four houses up from number fifty-seven. He knew Renee had a rear gate, like he did, as the two of them had sat on her small back porch a week or so ago with hot chocolates and discussed a recently released book of short stories.

Unlatching the gate, he slipped inside the back garden and made his way to the porch. He could see a light on in the hall but none in the kitchen, so he was able to get right up to the back door and peer in the kitchen window. He couldn't see anyone inside and everything looked normal. Matt turned the handle, expecting it to be locked, but the door opened silently. Taking a deep breath and reassuring himself that he could do this - Renee really needed him - he stepped inside, closing the door gently behind him.

He tiptoed through the kitchen, all the while listening for noises. He thought he heard something upstairs, but that could have been his imagination playing tricks. He moved into the hallway and paused. No sound coming from the living room, or anywhere else downstairs. Matt trod on the first stair. It made the tiniest of squeaks and he stopped in his tracks. He was sure if someone was in the house they would have heard that, but no one came, nothing moved, there was no sound. He took another step up and this time it was quiet. Slowly he proceeded up the stairs to the landing. Now he thought he heard movement from the main bedroom.

He knew Renee had an American style *Jack and Jill bathroom* between her bedroom and the spare room, so he thought it would be best to enter from there, rather than take the door from the landing. He worked his way along the short corridor and into the spare room. There was the bed he had helped her move in, made up nicely and a fresh vase of flowers stood on the nightstand. Matt crept to the connecting door and paused. He could hear something from the main bedroom, some sort of movement. Either footsteps or a cupboard door opening. He was overwhelmed with a sense of urgency to help the girl who had begged for his assistance on the answering machine. Gripping the baseball bat tightly in both hands he edged the door to the bathroom open with his foot.

He could vaguely make out the shower stall and toilet in the dim glow coming from the semi open door to Renee's bedroom. Inching forward, he could see the corner of the bed and he could make out a closet on the far wall, which appeared to have all its doors closed, which was a good thing - it was probably where Renee was hiding. He heard a louder sound. Someone pulling a drawer out of a dressing table, he guessed. He breathed deeply and from deep down inside he screamed, like a wailing banshee, and flung open the bathroom door.

"ARRGGHH," he hollered, and came shooting into the room, only to see a dark shape disappear out of the bedroom door and on to the landing. He screamed again, "Get out, get out, arrgghh!"

He heard footsteps pelting down the stairs now, then fading

away, into the hall, before he lost the sound of them. Quickly Matt threw open the door to the closet, "Are you ok?" he demanded of Renee.

"Y-y-y-yes. I think so," she replied timidly, still coming to terms with Matt standing over her with a baseball bat. "Ok, stay there," he replied, and shot off, racing towards the stairs.

Matt tore down the stairs and headed for the kitchen. He heard a banging noise coming from the closed front door, but he didn't have time for that, he raced to the back door. Suddenly he could see the man's shadow. He was crouching behind the kitchen door on the small back porch. The moonlight was behind him, so Matt could see his outline. It appeared as though he was holding a gun. Without a thought for his safety, he yanked the door open, grabbed the bat with two hands, and swung it with full force at the black shadow.

Two shots rang out. "Police! Put your weapon down!" a voice screamed in the dark. Matt couldn't quite work out where the voice was coming from. He knew he'd connected his bat with the person on the porch and that man now lay writhing on the ground. Matt realised he had hit his stomach on something, it was severely painful. He looked down and saw blood gushing from the gunshots that had ripped into his abdomen and his chest. He looked up and saw four policemen, coming towards him from the back garden.

"Put the bat down. Put it down now."

"Drop it!"

All these instructions were coming from the various policemen.

Matt peered at them. *Didn't they understand, he was the*

good guy, the bad guy was laying on the ground in pain from where Matt had walloped him with the baseball bat. Matt tried to move but his legs were frozen. He even tried pointing towards the guy dressed in black on the floor, but his arm didn't seem to work. He fell to his knees.

Within seconds he was on the ground, lying next to the man he had hit. He turned his head slightly and the last thing he saw, before fading into unconsciousness, was the police badge on a chain around the man's neck.

* * *

"What is the prognosis?" the detective was asking the doctor in charge of Mathew Preston's case.

"It's not great, I can tell you that. The first bullet penetrated the stomach, not irreparable damage, but the second nicked the aorta and there was severe internal bleeding. It was touch and go whether he'd pull through the operation, but he's stabilised now, and I am expecting a slow start to his recovery tonight," the doctor replied. "How is the police officer who got hit with the bat?"

"He'll live, but he's pretty bruised and battered. The kid managed to crack four ribs and the officer broke his ankle as he fell! Talk about a terrible state of affairs. Never seen anything like it in my twenty years in the force. The hero got shot, trying to do the right thing, but ended up attacking a police officer, who was also trying to do the right thing!" The detective shook his head. "We got the bastard who caused all this though. Idiot had left his getaway car up the street, with its lights on, so when the cops finally realised what was going on they found him trying to start his car, which had a flat battery. Nailed him on twelve burglaries across three suburbs, he still had all the stolen goods in the boot of his car. Truly, what a bloody galah!"

Detective Morrison assumed his position outside Mathew's room, relieving the young constable who had been sitting there most of the afternoon. He picked up a magazine and started flipping through it. It was going to be a long night, but he wanted to be here when the kid woke up. The detective had seen a lot of bad things happen to good people over the years, but his heart went out to this poor kid. Just a good Samaritan, in the wrong place at the wrong time.

Road Trip

He hummed a catchy tune that seemed appropriate as he cruised along the dusty, country road. *Take the Road Less Travelled* it was called.

He liked country music. It relaxed him and most of all he loved the stories they told. The singers sang of new lovers, old love gone wrong, doing it tough and persevering.

He particularly loved that song *King of the Road*. He felt the song was written about him. He was *King of the Road* today. Driving this highway, he felt invincible in his oversized Ford pickup truck.

He hated to admit it had been a little frantic at his last stop. That silly, interfering desk clerk knocking on the door just as he was finishing his clean up. If he had just been a couple of minutes later he would never have spotted the bucket with the bloody rags, or the plastic sheeting.

For goodness' sake, he thought, *don't people realise that motel guests do not want to be disturbed late at night. Especially by annoying desk clerks telling them that there is no breakfast service tomorrow as the cook has come down with the flu! Honestly, a simple note on the breakfast room door would have sufficed.* Still, it had turned out to be one of those rare two-for-one opportunities. He managed to get the weedy little guy to step inside the room, then he took care of him swiftly. It meant a hastier clean up session and departure from the motel much earlier than normal. He was forced to leave during the night and missed his usual peaceful sleep-in and mid-morning departure.

Daniel's thoughts drifted back to earlier that evening.

She had been a cutie with a gorgeous smile. A little skinny for his personal taste, but beggars can't be choosers, can they? He snickered out loud at the irony. He had chosen her, that was for sure.

He loved her hair though. The colour was a pretty shade of auburn and it was so soft and long. She must have used an apple-based shampoo, because even now he could smell that fresh apple scent on his fingers. He'd probably spent the best part of an hour brushing her hair once the Klonopin started to take effect.

He thought she had probably enjoyed it. It was quite likely that no-one had brushed her hair for her in a long time. He guessed she must have been about twenty and wondered when mothers stopped brushing their daughters' hair? Maybe when they reached high school age. It was then that they started to exert their own will. Most girls would probably start objecting to their mothers being involved in their personal grooming around that time. They began to form their own opinions then, and as he knew from personal experience, they started to have their first taste of puberty, particularly sexual urges.

He broke through his reverie to focus on the intersection up ahead. As he remembered it, he needed to take the main road that curved off to the left, then it should only be about two more hours to Spencerville.

He felt a little tingling sensation spread through his loins. Spencerville. He had been looking forward to this one for quite some time.

It had been twenty-three years since he went to middle school there, and he knew from his research just how much it had grown. Now there was an all-girls school and a convent in town.

He had secured himself a room at the local Best Western motel, mentioning that he was a corporate salesman and booking the conference room for fake 'business meetings' all day. He was adept at setting up a nice little alibi for himself. He smiled into the rear-view mirror, confident and pleased at his clever ruse.

Take the Road Less Travelled he sang, an eerie smirk spreading across his face. He turned up the radio and planted his foot more heavily on the accelerator, eager now to reach his destination and partake in his next adventure.

"Breaking news just in," the female newscaster interrupted his song, "Binghamton police have just informed us that two bodies have been discovered at a local motel. Police have security camera footage from a bank across the road. They are currently looking for a Caucasian man, 175cm tall, brown hair with a very distinctive scar across his left cheek. He is believed to be wearing blue overalls, a red check shirt, black bandana and joggers. The suspect was last seen driving a red

Ford pickup truck, licence plate FGR 6795 ..."

There was a horrendous screech of brakes and after swerving off the road the pickup rolled several times. It eventually came to rest at the base of an old oak tree and burst into a huge fireball. The final thought that flashed through Daniel's mind as the life ebbed out of his mangled body was... Damn, I should have taken the road to the right, not the left. *The Road Less Travelled.*

Garbage men

Dusk was falling. It seemed to be taking forever. David went through his bag again, although this would be his fourth go. Another twenty minutes and it would be time to leave.

Duct tape – check. Hand-cuffs – check. Timer, knife, lock pick – check, check, check. *Don't tell me I forgot the disposable gloves* he thought, then, turning the bag sideways, he spied the packet tucked inside and breathed a sigh of relief.

He walked to the chest of drawers, picked up his scarf and coat from the back of the chair and put them on. He ticked off a mental checklist as the minutes slowly passed: map, gloves, envelope full of papers, torch. The truck was full of petrol. All good. Putting on his warm, outdoor gloves, he picked up the bag and exited down the stairs.

"I'm off, mum, see you tomorrow morning," he called out as he went down the hall, past the living room where his mother, Doris, was knitting in the chair watching the news on the telly.

"I packed your supper, David, it's on the hall table. I put in a thermos of coffee too – we don't want you falling asleep on the job now, do we? Stay safe, love," his mother called back.

David stopped, picked up his thermos, and his lunch pail, filled with homemade goodies. This made him smile. How many hitmen had their mother make their supper for them when they went out to a job? Not many, would be his bet. He closed the door quietly, locking it to keep his mother safe. A man in his profession knows just how important home security really is.

He walked quickly down the village street. Crossing the cobblestones, he almost stepped on old Mr Jones's cat, which was curled up near the bushes on the sidewalk. The little ball of fur sat there most nights, waiting for his master to stagger home from the local pub on the next corner. He quickened his step as he passed the shop fronts, all closed for the night, and turned into the street where the three warehouses at the back of the village were located.

David had congratulated himself last year on his forethought, when one of the little outbuildings near the warehouse came up for rent. He had secured it for a minimal monthly payment. A while back he had bought himself an old Ford pickup and a little Morris Minor for a few hundred dollars cash. He housed both vehicles there, and only drove them when it was dark. As far as he knew no-one was aware they were parked there, but even if they were discovered, without a licence or papers in his name, no-one could connect them to him. He had secured the unit by telephone and mail and posted off a money order each month from a neighbouring town for the rent. The rental company had been more than happy with the four months' rent up front he'd sent them - they hadn't even asked to sight ID.

The truck started quietly, belying its beat-up appearance on the outside. Although it looked old, and blended well with local farm vehicles, it was meticulously maintained, spotless inside, with all lights in working order, and David drove carefully. It would not be good for him to be picked up for speeding, or some other minor traffic infringement, not in his line of work.

It would only take him a half hour to Harrisburg, the neighbouring town, and there he would pick up Phil, his accomplice for this job.

He didn't usually take on these bigger jobs, he didn't like having to involve someone else. However, it paid exceptionally well, and due to the family consisting of five members, he would need an extra set of hands. He had used Phil a few times before, without too much trouble. Admittedly he did tend to talk too much. David always found it better to keep communications simple, direct and brief. In and out under twenty minutes, that was the plan. Last time he used Phil he had chatted with the mark, for God's sakes. It meant a delay of nearly ten minutes! You really needed to de-personalise in this job. You couldn't go getting *involved* with the target!

You weren't employed to make decisions, they were already made. You weren't there to hold court with them, you were just there to carry out your mission. It was paid work. Someone had to do it. Not everyone could be florists or wedding planners. Some folk had to work in the not-so-pleasant industries, paid to take out the garbage. For some it meant emptying septic tanks of effluent; for others it meant removing dead bodies from morgues or hospitals. David was paid to remove human garbage that had no place in civilised society.

He would get his instructions, via mail sent from the organisation in London. He had his own set boundaries, three counties across and four counties down. He would follow the instructions as set out in his job outline package. This would include the names of the targets, the charges against them, a few paragraphs on the mark's lifestyle, routine, schedules etc.

David would do a short recon mission, two days prior to the job date, and that would usually be enough to work out how to get the job done.

Occasionally there would be a bigger job, like this one. One where the whole family was involved. The target this time was a slave-trader organisation, with ties to prostitution. The grandfather, father, mother and two boys aged twenty-seven and twenty-four lived in a house on a garden estate in the better part of the city, just fifty miles south of David's village.

They would be returning tonight from a so-called 'family holiday' in Asia, where they had not been sightseeing like tourists, but had been organising a branch of their business, headed up by a crime lord who worked out of Hong Kong.

The family would arrive in two town cars from the airport, and only the manservant would be in the house. The plans had changed at the last minute (no doubt engineered by the organisation), so the other staff were not expecting the family to return until the morning and would not be on duty until then. The job outline explained that the family would return at approximately 3am, due to delays at the airport with their baggage and customs, no doubt also orchestrated by the organisation.

They would be tired from a twice-delayed, long flight and the best time to strike would be just after their arrival home, when they would be tired and preparing for bed, and their guard would be at its lowest.

David and Phil discussed the plan as they travelled together towards the city. David would take out the alarm system - for which he had a complete schematic diagram - and enter through the back door off the conservatory. Phil would come into the house through the kitchen, which had a large dog door installed for the two Doberman guard dogs, Prince and Lord. The dogs had both come down with a mystery illness three days ago and had been in the local vet hospital. They were both returning home tomorrow, all fit and healthy, because that was when the family was due back too. David had long ago learned the best way to deal with guard dogs was to remove them from the equation, but he would certainly never condone any unnecessary violence or harm to a defenceless animal.

David would find the manservant and overpower him, leaving him tied up in the pantry while he carried out his business. The boys lived in the downstairs rooms, towards the back of the house, and both had a private ensuite where David would find them, and take care of each one, while they were showering. It was their standard practice to shower immediately upon returning from any travel they undertook.

Phil would use the servants' stairs from the kitchen to the

first floor, where the mother and father had separate wings. He would take the left one first, to find the father. It was highly probable he would be reclining in his study with a stiff drink, opening his mail, checking his emails and other business-related matters. Phil should have no problem disposing of him in the study, as his desk faced the window and he wouldn't even see Phil coming. He would then make his way down the hall to the mother's suite and dispose of her. There would be little doubt she would already be asleep, as she was not one for good hygiene habits, and having consumed copious quantities of the free alcohol on the plane, (arranged and supplied by the organisation, once again) she would not be in any state to resist.

It would be a quick and easy task, and then he would head up to the third floor to the grandfather's suite. Phil should have even less of a problem there, as by this time the grandfather would have completed his ablutions and be in bed.

He would have his hearing aid switched off and removed for the night, and his glasses in their case on the bedside table. He wouldn't be capable of hearing or seeing anything untoward.

In total it should take Phil no longer than nine minutes and then he would return to the kitchen where they would meet up. David, having completed his tasks with the family, would have moved to the main office at the front of the house, where he'd leave the envelope addressed to Superintendent Hastings of the International Crime section of the CID, in a central spot, possibly on the large oak desk facing the window.

All in all, they should be in and out in a maximum of fifteen to seventeen minutes.

David pulled the truck into the shady lane that ran the length of the property. There were no cameras reaching this side wall as it was over seven-foot-high, and the security guards obviously thought the attack dogs, and the height of the wall, would be enough to discourage intruders from this direction. David got his bag out of the boot, then locked up, while Phil unfurled the grappling hook. Within seconds he had it secured to an oak tree on the other side of the wall and was halfway up before David joined him. The men were over and down the other side noiselessly.

They paused then to take stock, David nodding to Phil as he confirmed the town cars were pulling away, and the family were all inside the house. They waited a few more minutes before Phil left to go to his entry point, leaving David to pick the lock and begin his tasks, as planned.

Disarming the security cameras took less time than expected, and he set the timer for twenty minutes as usual, putting it down, out of view, near the back door. He set the timer on his watch as well and headed off to where he could hear the manservant bringing in cases from the front porch. He dealt with him swiftly, silently and methodically. It was not in the instructions to hurt this man in any way, in fact, it had been made clear that this employee was innocent in this scenario. He had only been with the family for two months and as far as the organisation was concerned it believed he had no knowledge of the underhanded, repulsive practices this family business engaged in. David secured him and placed him in the pantry, as per the plan, and continued with the rest of his duties.

After exactly eleven minutes he had completed his part of the job and headed back to the kitchen to the rendezvous.

At twelve minutes David began to get a little anxious, and by thirteen minutes he was feeling stirrings of concern. Phil turned up just on fourteen minutes.

They did not speak but David could see worry across Phil's face, and gave him a reassuring pat on the arm. His accomplice nodded at him and the men took one last glance around, David picked up the timer and his duffle bag and they left, securing the back door as they went.

Neither man spoke until they had got over the wall, stacked their things into the boot and driven off down the lane.

"All good buddy?" David asked Phil.

"Had a bit of trouble upstairs. The old geezer was still awake. He was sitting in a chair, the picture of a loving old grandfather, reading Dickens by lamplight – bloody Norah. It just tugged at my heart strings a bit, you know," Phil said falteringly. David looked across at him. Phil continued, "I know, I know. I need to toughen up a bit. I remembered what you said last time and I quickly brought up those pictures on my phone. The ones you gave me of the dead girl in the alley and the babies and the children begging on the streets because their mums were taken away from them by traffickers. It worked too. I was able to look at this guy completely differently then. The scum. He saw me coming but was way too slow to do anything about it." Phil took a deep breath. "Anyways, it got done. All finished. Another point to the good guys." He turned and looked out the window to the darkness.

David drove to their favourite spot by the river. The little parking bay where you could see the city lights in the distance. He turned the engine off and brought out the lunch box and thermos. Phil retrieved paper cups from the glove compartment, and they sat in silence and ate their supper.

"Well, another day, another dollar. I'd best be dropping you off and then getting home to Mother," David said, packing the rubbish away from their supper into a plastic bag.

The men put the lunch pail and thermos away and David drove Phil home.

As he got out of the truck with his backpack, he grabbed the plastic bag from the front floor. "Want me to take out the garbage?" he asked David.

The men laughed. "Yes please," Dave replied, "you'd make a great garbage man." They laughed again, and Phil closed the door and went inside his apartment.

David drove the truck back to the warehouse and then strolled home. He let himself in quietly, and took a long, hot shower, scrubbing himself clean, then laying in his bed.

His last thought as he drifted off...*yes, we do make very good garbage men...* and he slept the sleep of the just, for a full eight hours.

Networking Dinners

It began as a perfectly normal 'networking' type function. A few beers with like-minded people, a bit of a get together on a Friday evening to unwind. No one wanted to get rolling drunk or cause a scene. It was still fresh on everyone's mind how quickly they needed to go into recovery mode after the last event got out of hand. Those young fellows who got themselves drunk and stoned. Wandering off, down the mountain, past the retreat boundaries and into the local township. They had made complete fools of themselves at the local tavern, then followed the barmaid home after closing, and when she cut through the park, they'd jumped her. Securing her to the ornamental sundial with their ties and belts and having their way with her. Over and over, apparently, she was kept there for nearly two hours, completely at their mercy.

It had caused a huge problem and the group at Taylor's Retreat were forced to deny they even knew the boys to avoid being dragged into the whole sordid mess. They certainly couldn't afford to jeopardise their clandestine meetings at Mount Versace, here in the backwaters of Texas.

It was true, old Mr Taylor had warned them, letting young ones become members was fraught with danger, he'd advised. "They will be our undoing," he'd said. Well, perhaps the Networkers should have paid heed. As he had prophesised these young men had very nearly done exactly that.

The elders managed to keep it all contained of course. Cash was required to change hands, semi-anonymously, and a couple of breaking news stories were engineered. Combined with some well spread rumours the whole unfortunate event had died down. The girl had 'transferred' out of town to Dallas and after a small windfall was doing quite well in college. The young men had been dispensed with and were no longer part of the Networkers organisation. Over a period of a few weeks the locals had forgotten about it, their minds on the large anonymous donation to improve the local swimming pool, and the information that the town was up for nomination in the state tidy towns awards.

Still, no point in risking it again, that's why tonight's event was a little lower key. They had started with a few drinks as usual, a couple of light cocktails, before taking their seats at the table for the evening's festivities…beginning with the dinner.

The rostered host, Boris, and his wife Mavis, had done a marvellous job with the decorating this month. A medieval theme. The table set up in the main hall, the windows all covered with rich burgundy, thick brocade drapes. The chairs were brought in especially. Tall, high backed, wooden, with plush red velvet seats.

The two heavy wooden tables they had purchased a few

months ago matched perfectly and as they took their places around the table he noticed everyone had really got into the theme, turning up in their medieval finery.

Boris and Mavis, as befitting the hosts, took their rightful place at the head of the table, and the other three elders and their partners, himself, his wife Trudy, Marcus and Maude and John and his partner Billy all sat to their right and left. At the top end of the table. The other six couples were seated in order of seniority, as was standard in an organisation as important and traditional as theirs. The waiters tonight – Joanne and Sheryl - were the wives of the newest members and looked appropriate in their 'buxom wenches' attire. All in all, a grand display he thought as he surveyed the scene.

The table itself was resplendent, with silver wine goblets and antique flatware, polished until it sparkled. The napkins were hand embroidered with a red blood drop appliquéd in each corner, co-ordinating with the curtains perfectly. Yes, Mavis and Boris would have to be recognised for this achievement. The meticulous attention to detail making the Medieval March Madness feast an appropriate title for the culinary wizardry in which they were about to partake.

First course had been beautifully decorated hors d'oeuvres on silver platters, brought out for each couple to share, and had consisted of liver pâté and kidney dips, accompanied by wafer thin slices of crispy skin, they went down perfectly. A fitting appetiser to the sumptuous main – a genuine, full-bodied roast that was carved at the table! Mavis had set the table so that the other end had been left free of guests, table and glassware. This was evidently where they intended to lay the platter carrying the beautiful Laura – the golden-haired beauty chosen at last month's dinner from the catalogue they received each quarter from their supplier in Germany. She had been a leggy girl, not exactly buxom, but with a long, full head of blonde hair, a natural blonde too he noted with a smile of approval.

Carved Memento

Barry scowled. The sky was a revolting blue, the sun causing everything to shine and reflect into his eyes. This was why he liked to work at night! He hated having to be outside in the daylight hours. Right now, he would much prefer to be in his basement, windowless and gloomy, working on his carved mementos. He let his mind wander to his little creations. They were special, unique, and they helped define him. Barry was legendary in these parts, not as the crazy loon at the end of the road who slept all day and worked all night, although he was sure he had heard that mentioned a couple of times, but as a master craftsman. If you walked past his house late at night you would hear the dulcet tones of his classical music playing. His taste tended to run to the more menacing or ominous tunes, providing what he considered to be a melodious background to the sound of his carving tools.

He hurried back to the car with his arms full of supplies. Why the wood yard and the hobby shop did not have online stores, with home delivery, was beyond him. Nowadays you should be able to get everything you wanted, delivered, simply with a computer and a credit card.

Barry was in a hurry to get home. He tossed his supplies into the car and then took the shortest route. While obeying the law, he did sit right on the speed limit, and might possibly have stopped for that orange light, if he hadn't been so eager to get back.

Turning into his driveway at last, he hit the button on the remote clipped to the sun visor and waited irritably for the roller door to go up. "Hurry up, hurry up," he mumbled. Once the door had closed behind him Barry felt his shoulders relax and the tension ease from the base of his neck. *That's better*, he smiled to himself, *home sweet home*. Although usually a man who felt quite safe and secure in his home, he still double-checked that the remote-controlled door had shut properly.

Taking his supplies with him, he unlocked the connecting door to the kitchen, turning to lock it again after he had come through. "You can never be too careful, there are a lot of crazies out there," he said, chuckling reassuringly to no-one in particular.

After placing his bags on the kitchen counter, he disarmed the security system - setting it to 'home', which meant he could walk around inside with ease and there was no risk of the motion detectors setting off the alarm. However, he would still be notified if there was a breach in the perimeter of his house, including windows, doors and exterior gates.

He shot a glance towards the bank of security monitors attached to outside cameras that covered every direction around his home. Seeing nothing untoward, he continued down the six stairs to the basement, carrying two of his bags and a bottle of water he'd grabbed from the fridge as he went past.

His mind was already racing ahead to the next carving he had planned. He had finished the drawings yesterday, so he would be able to start on the wood model today. Once that was complete, he would be ready to do the final carving, his *piece de resistance*. Barry put the bags off to one side and unrolled the intricate, very precise drawing on his desk, securing it down with some wood carving tools - tools that had long ago belonged to his father, and his father before him.

He remembered the advice his father used to give him as a boy sitting on a stool, watching those arthritic hands clasping the awl or the chisel. Using this equipment Daddy would carve beautiful musical instruments, a cello or a violin, a fiddle or a guitar. He would turn them out perfectly, his musician clients often saying they could 'hear the love' he had put into making their tools of trade for them.

"Barry," his father would say, "You must learn to respect the wood. The tree it came from has spent years growing for you, so you must treat it gently and with care, like you would a lover. You must learn to measure twice and cut once so there is no wastage. You should always try to put a little bit of yourself into every carving."

Well he had certainly mastered all that over the past thirty years, in fact, he grinned, he had been able to take it a step further...

He stole a glance over to the other side of the room where his other work-table stood - the table with the materials all laid out neatly, in precise rows waiting for his hands, his loving, caressing hands, that would carefully chip away, shaping, smoothing and moulding until the miniature musical instrument took shape.

You see, Barry considered himself a conductor, of sorts. He was a fine craftsman, making all the musical instruments required for his own orchestra. The main difference being that they were just one twentieth the size of real instruments.

However, what made these instruments even more special was that they were all carved from pieces of bone, human bone. While most craftsmen would use wood or ceramic or stone to carve, Barry chose this special medium for a reason. Each bone came from someone who had been involved with changing the direction of Barry's life over fifteen years ago.

For a while Barry had enjoyed following in his dad's footsteps, turning and carving wood first as a hobby when a child, and later, as a teenager, being apprenticed to his father every day after school. However, his one passion, above all else, was to play the cello.

He had begged his father to make him a cello for his ninth birthday and he had practised at home, late at night in the back shed, soundproofing it with egg cartons, painstakingly collected by his mother over many months, and attached by Barry to the walls and roof. Finally, when he felt he was good enough, he had joined the school band. This was in his first year in high school. He had loved his band lessons and rehearsal sessions, not missing one. He practised until his fingers literally bled, and then, in his third high school year, he spoke to his parents about trying out for the semi-professional orchestra in Pittsburgh.

His parents had scoffed a little, but his father had finally relented, with the stipulation that it did not interfere with his work in the family business.

For a year Barry attended every one of his school classes and worked evenings and weekends at Silver & Son, Fine Wood Craftsmen, just as he promised his father he would. On top of that he devoted every spare minute to his passion, improving his musical skills. Then, fifteen years ago the all-important moment arrived, just like a finely tuned orchestral crescendo. Everything Barry had done had led up to this, the auditions for the Pittsburgh Symphony Orchestra.

He had attained the age of sixteen, as required. He had his own instrument, a fine cello his dad had taken nearly a year to make for him. He had passed his eighth-grade music exam and now he had an appointment for his audition at 9.30am Saturday 7th August 2002.

Barry could still remember the excitement he felt as he made a great effort to groom himself immaculately and dress perfectly for the audition.

He arrived fifteen minutes early with his mother. Being under the age of twenty-one he still required a guardian to attend with him. He remembered sitting on plastic chairs, lined up against the wall, nervously awaiting his turn and when it finally came, he was not as frightened as he thought he might be. Barry entered the audition room and spent the next twenty-five minutes playing his heart out. Moreover, he did it exceptionally well.

In the following ten minutes he had to answer questions relating to music, his skills and aptitude. He answered them truthfully, explaining how he had studied, worked as his father's apprentice and attended his music lessons and band practice for the past eight years. He was almost finished when the gentleman on the end of the panel, Mr Wiseman from the council, seemed to sneer at him and asked, "So, if chosen in my orchestra (he turned out to be the conductor, although Barry didn't know that at the time) you will obviously have to give up your part-time job Mr Silver." The man continued. "My boys don't have time for school, orchestra AND working in a shop. You do understand that the orchestra MUST be your first priority, don't you?"

Barry had never had to lie before. He knew that everything rested on his answer to this question.

"Umm, yes sir. Of course. The orchestra would definitely be my first priority sir." Barry's voice was shaky, and he had secretly crossed his fingers behind his back while answering.

It was a week to the day after the audition that Barry's mom received the letter in the mail.

The panel regretted to inform them that Barry was not deemed suitable to join the orchestra at this time. Mother broke it to him gently, alone in his bedroom, so that he was not embarrassed in front of his father, but still he had sobbed, and she had held him while he cried.

It had taken months to get over the incident and he had tried out again for the next two years, both times receiving the same letter. By the third year, Mr Wiseman the conductor, had retired from his position as conductor. However, he still sat on the adjudicating panel and he seemed to be continually sneering at Barry during his auditions.

Barry had moved on of course. Graduating from school, working in his dad's business as he was expected to do. It was over fourteen years later that he discovered, purely by chance, what had led to his receiving those letters of rejection, and ultimately the events that had directed the rest of his life plan.

Apparently, Mr Wiseman's son Nigel was a bit of a troublemaker back in the day. At the time Mr Wiseman was the school's music teacher and on the board of the Orchestra.

The boy, Nigel, had found it difficult to study and had dropped out of school when he was just sixteen to join a local rock band. He had pressured his father into getting an expensive guitar made, by Barry's dad.

Young Nigel had managed to turn his life around eventually. After a couple of years of somewhat roguish behaviour, he secured a good job and married a local girl. He still played guitar, but his music of choice was now ballads and folk songs instead of head-banging rock and roll.

In 2001 there was a vacancy for a guitarist with the Pittsburgh Symphony Orchestra, so Nigel decided to try out for the position. At the audition all was going well until Nigel lost concentration for just a second and struck a particularly ear-piercing wrong note. It had caused the panel of adjudicators to grimace and wince and ultimately reject him for the position of guitarist.

As Mr Wiseman was not present at the audition (that would have been considered poor form) he only had Nigel's account of what had happened, and sadly Nigel had not been altogether truthful about the incident. The young man had been extremely embarrassed about his performance and had made a beeline straight for the men's room after exiting the Heinz Hall audition room. He had proceeded to knock his guitar several times on the basin and had busted two strings while doing so. On the way home Nigel had conjured up a story of how he had the misfortune of two strings breaking during the performance, and because of the poor quality of the workmanship of Silver and Son, he had not been able to complete the audition.

Well, word soon got around town that Silver & Son were not the 'Fine Wood Craftsmen' they purported to be, and Barry's father's business took a turn for the worse.

His father struggled to make ends meet for many years and eventually passed away in a drink-driving accident. Regrettably he took Barry's mother with him.

Barry had been just twenty-two when he had been forced to take over the business completely, and he had spent the last eight years building up Silver & Son, Fine Wood Craftsmen's reputation again.

Finally, now, in 2018 he could walk down the street and hold his head up high again. He had built up a large customer base, many of whom played instruments in a local or national orchestra. Barry and the business had been written up in the local papers, and there was even an article written in the Pittsburgh Post-Gazette commending the fine work of Silver & Son over the years, making instruments for famous musicians.

However, nothing Barry managed to achieve had repaired the broken heart he had suffered from being turned down for the orchestra as a young sixteen-year-old musician. Over the years his anger had festered and bubbled, deep down inside, until one day a couple of months ago, it had erupted, like a volcano.

It was when he had overheard a conversation outside the stadium while delivering a replacement instrument to one of the performers. He'd been sitting in his car with the window wound down, filling in some paperwork, when a van had pulled up near-by. An ensemble of musicians alighted and hung around for a smoke, and Barry heard their conversation turn to how life can be so unfair for musicians. One man asked, "What about that girl who was refused a position in the orchestra for Swan Lake because she was gay?"

"They said it was for her 'lack of ability to follow instructions' but we all know the conductor was a devout Christian and would not have been able to handle having a gay lead violinist!" another replied.

"Yeah, and that kid from Silver's, remember? He didn't end up getting a place on the symphony orchestra because that old guy Wiseman hated his dad," the first man continued.

"I remember that. All because of Wiseman's son, Neville. No, that's not right. Nigel, yeah, that was his name. He blew his audition and lied to his father, blaming old man Silver for an inferior piece of equipment," another musician chimed in.

"Yeah, I heard he even poisoned the adjudicating panel for the next few years," said the older guy, leaning against the fence. "Told them there was no way old Harry Silver would support his kid being in the orchestra. Said he couldn't run his business without him, so they voted no on him for three years running. That kid was a child prodigy too, I've heard.

Taught himself to play. Wonder what happened to him?"

"He took over from his dad. He's still got Silver & Son on Grantham Street, but he does most of the work from home I think. Turning out some great instruments too, but it's a shame if he really did have a talent the world missed out on." The men stubbed out their cigarette butts and sauntered inside.

Barry had taken a while to process what the men had said and over the coming weeks had not been able to contain his anger. He had done some research and found old Mr Wiseman, residing in an assisted living facility outside the city. He located Nigel Wiseman too, divorced now and living in some hovel in the 'ghetto' part of town.

It had taken time of course. Barry spent nearly a month building up rapport with a nurse at Jacaranda Lodge and during that time he had managed to duplicate her key to the staff entrance. He'd learned about their slack record-keeping processes too. One dark and stormy night, using the thunder and heavy rain as cover, he slipped into the facility undetected. He made a quick detour to the office to alter the name and a couple of other details on the old man's file, then he made short work of taping the mouth of the sleeping Mr Wiseman, sitting him up in a wheel chair and wheeling him out to the staff car park, where he knew the security cameras hadn't worked for some time.

He'd taken him home and kept the old man sedated in the basement, shackled to a chain hooked around the furnace, Barry then turned his attention to Nigel. That had taken only a couple of days of reconnaissance. He'd watched the guy shuffle down to the unemployment office, play chess in the park, then return home and spend the day and night dozing in a chair in front of re-runs of Law and Order.

He'd waited until the day after Nigel received his unemployment cheque and had purchased two bottles of beer. By 7 o'clock Nigel was snoring. In his drunken stupor he'd left the door unlocked (certainly not an unusual occurrence) and the TV was up nice and loud. Barry had got in and out within fifteen minutes. He'd secured Nigel, turned the volume down a bit so it could play all day and night and locked the door on his way out. No-one would even notice he was gone until next month's rent day. Even then it would probably take a couple of weeks for anyone to come knocking.

He'd kept the men alive in the basement for three days, lecturing them daily about the wrongs they had committed - how the poor decisions they had made, when lying and influencing others had affected the outcomes of many other people's lives. He made them aware of how Barry and his family had suffered.

Finally, Barry put them to sleep permanently and sealed them in purpose-built, odour-proof caskets with the eggs of 200 Dermestidae beetles. Within three weeks the larvae had hatched and done their job. The men's flesh had been removed and all that remained were their bones. He then exterminated the beetles humanely and proceeded to boil the men's bones until they were shiny and clean.

It had taken another twenty-four hours for the whitening process – bleaching them using a 4% hydrogen peroxide solution. Barry had read extensively about the process and knew the dangers of using chlorine bleach as this would cause the bones to crumble and decay. The bones were then left to air dry for a few days in sunlight. He had kept them protected from predators by laying them in a bird cage on the back porch.

That afternoon Barry finished the final piece of his bone orchestra – the miniature cello. He brought all the pieces carefully upstairs. He had cleared a space on the middle shelf of the book case, where a white urn stood at one end and a brown one at the other. He laid out the tiny instruments as they would be arranged in a proper orchestra and sat back to admire his handiwork.

"You'd be proud of me Daddy," he said to the brown urn. "I did this for you and Mom." His gaze rested sadly on the white urn.

After admiring his handiwork Barry sat back in his arm chair and turned on the news.

"An elderly man has gone missing from Jacaranda Lodge, an assisted-living facility. Authorities believe that there had been some confusion regarding his being signed out of the premises in the log book three days ago. However, there are now grave fears for his life due to his dressing gown being discovered near the Allegheny River, just a short walk across the field opposite the facility. According to the manager, records show Mr Henry Whiteman was eighty-nine years old and had no known living relatives."

Barry dozed in the chair, a contented smile across his face. It was the best sleep he'd had in years.

Bad Luck

He was getting tired. He'd been cruising downtown for at least an hour. *That's the problem on these winter's nights,* he thought. *No one wants to come out and play.* Not the working girls nor the johns. It's a 'Catch 22' situation. Without the clients, what was the point in the girls standing on corners, huddling against the wind and rain? But the paying customers certainly weren't going to come out in this weather, not if they were limited for choice.

Silas Crawley was a deviant. He would be the first to admit it. But he did have standards. He wouldn't touch the young ones, that just wouldn't be right. He'd never go near the newbies, mainly because he still had hope that they would be able to turn their lives around. No, it was the older, trashed ones that he made a beeline for. The ones who'd been in the game a long time. Those with drug and alcohol addictions, they were his prey.

Although, you could hardly call them 'prey', when you were doing the world a favour. Prey had such nasty connotations, didn't it? I mean, a farmer who was eradicating rabbits that ruined his crops would not refer to the errant

167

bunnies as prey. A gardener sprinkling slug pellets to save his flowers would not be condemned. What about a local council who engaged a team of shark cullers to protect its beaches and residents? They wouldn't be looked down upon for carrying out their duties, would they? No, they would be praised for looking out for the welfare of others. And that's exactly how he saw himself. A protector of humanity, a clean-up squad of one. A man whose job it was to rid downtown of the vermin who tainted this once lively area, full of theatres and nightclubs and family-friendly restaurants.

Silas pulled up outside the boarded-up Palace Theatre. Not much was left of the old gal now. Her windows were plywood, nailed up at all sorts of weird angles. It reminded him of the patchwork on his grandma's quilt which adorned the bed in his basement, where he brought the women. The theatre's beautiful double glass doors had been smashed and ripped off their hinges many years ago. A gaping hole where they used to stand, so regal and majestic, may have looked inviting to vagrants, but he knew that once inside you ran the gauntlet of standing on used syringes, meth pipes and filthy garbage.

Damn this rain. It had been continuous all night. Not only did it make it difficult to see but it was making him desperate for the bathroom. He'd already had a 'comfort stop' an hour ago at a hamburger place on Third Ave. He pulled over to the curb, just up from the theatre. Glancing up and down both sides of the street, he couldn't see a soul. There had been a girl in the doorway of the old bakery up near the corner when he'd cruised past earlier, but she had disappeared. Either she had found a customer and was now in the back seat of a car or in a cheap motel, or she'd had enough and gone home for the night. He locked the car and jogged across to the doorway, took one more look around and entered the dark, abandoned building. He stood still for a full minute so that his eyes would adjust to the gloom and he could get his bearings. He hadn't been in here for years, but he remembered a foyer that had a set of toilets off to the left. The urinals might still be there, and he'd feel better about using them than peeing on the floor, like an animal.

He made his way cautiously towards the rear of the foyer, past the defunct candy bar and entered under the archway that lead to the restrooms. It was dark in the hallway, but the windows set up high, near the ceiling, threw an eerie greenish light across the wall. A street light behind the old oak tree in the park across the road spread its filtered light into the derelict building.

Silas found the men's room easily enough, it was the one doorway with no door. He trod carefully over beer cans, cool drink bottles made into cheap bongs, food wrappers and a couple of dead rodents. The men's room, while stinking like a pile of rotting garbage on a 40° day, still had urinals along one wall and two lonely looking porcelain toilet bowls. They were without lids, walls, or cisterns but that didn't bother him tonight. One of them had what looked like a Royal Doulton cup, minus the handle, sitting on top. That made him smile - the irony of such an exquisite piece of china, broken and sitting atop a rotting toilet. He chose the urinal and unzippered.

Silas finished and made his way back through the foyer. As he passed the candy bar he gasped. Something had come hurtling through the open doorway and skittered to a halt, shattering on a discarded brick inches from his feet.

Whoosh!

Flames shot upwards and outwards, catching Silas off guard. Fire seemed to overwhelm him, as much of the liquid from the Molotov cocktail had splashed on to his shoes, pants and along the edge of his long, winter jacket. For a few seconds he was rooted to the spot. His brain was unable to catch up with what he was seeing and experiencing.

Silas vaguely remembered some fire training from his army reserve days…stop, drop and roll. He flung himself on the floor, straight on to a pile of newspapers and leaves that the homeless had been using to sleep on, and within seconds the dry, combustible material completely engulfed him in flames.

* * *

The fire brigade turned up, eventually. There didn't seem much of a reason for the usual rush and urgency when the fire was in an abandoned building at that end of town.

It took them nearly an hour and a half to get the blaze under control, and once it was safe enough to enter the building they found Silas Crawley lying in the foyer.

"Well, this guy is toast," one of the firemen commented to Detective Saunders who would be investigating the case if it turned out to be anything other than an accident.

"Looks like another piece of the Molotov Vigilante's handiwork," he added.

Arson squad detectives had been called on to investigate seven fires over the past four months, which they attributed to a criminal they had dubbed the 'Molotov Vigilante'. Generally, his MO was the same in each case. He would hit an abandoned building (shops, restaurants and warehouses) in the downtown precinct. All were notorious hangouts for vagrants and the homeless, and were often locations used for drug deals, sometimes drug storage. This guy would drive past, throw a firebomb inside, and burn the place to the ground. An email would arrive at the local police station the following morning claiming responsibility and telling law enforcement authorities not to bother to thank him as it was thanks enough to know that he was responsible for cleaning up yet another ghetto that enticed people to sleep on the streets and participate in the underworld of drugs.

The unsub appeared to have a real grudge against vagrants, itinerants and anyone involved with drugs. He mentioned in one email that he would never hit community-run flop houses, homeless shelters or soup kitchens run by local church groups. He totally believed they were providing an essential service to those genuinely in need.

Detective Saunders spent the next week investigating the fire at the old Palace Theatre. He managed to identify the victim, Silas Crawley, although it still puzzled him as to what a man who ran his own profitable hardware store, lived a quiet, solitary life in a little house out in the suburbs at the base of the hills, would be doing inside the old building. The detective interviewed neighbours, Silas's employees and although there was no family to speak of, he did find a distant cousin who filled him in on Silas's life as much as he knew. Saunders gathered the man had led a quiet, hardworking life. He had married Trixie, his true love just seven years ago and she had passed away last year. According to the cousin, unbeknown to Silas, she had led a double life during their marriage and had prostituted herself to feed a drug addiction that had started long before they met.

Detective Saunders was a diligent police officer and investigated Trixie and confirmed the story the cousin had told him. The employees had added that their boss had 'shut down' since his wife passed, and these past few months they had noticed he was continually tired, occasionally late for work and often distracted. He concluded from this that Trixie's death had led Silas to turn to prostitutes to fill his sexual needs, but there really wasn't anything particularly suspicious about that. Sadly, it was a fact of life that these girls filled a need for some men, who, for whatever reason, could not face normal relationships.

He had searched Silas's home, and his workplace, and other than an unusual plastic covered rollaway bed, stored in the basement, and a pair of shackles attached to a chain on the floor next to that bed, the detective didn't find anything out of the ordinary. There was nothing to indicate that Silas was any more than an unlucky passer-by who had perhaps been caught short and had slipped into the building to relieve himself at exactly the moment when the Molotov Vigilante had struck.

Detective Saunders felt sad when he considered how little we really knew of people's lives and how they lived them. He had always favoured openness and honesty in his own personal relationships and found this had benefitted him well over the years. He pondered the complexities of fate and *bad luck* as he closed the folder, stacking it on top of the others to go to the Arson Squad archives, to be filed as another unsolved case.

Jude St Clair

The author lives in Mandurah, Western Australia. She has a Bachelor of Commerce, majoring in Marketing and Management, which she obtained as a mature age student while raising her family of four children. She loves to read and write and with her partner has been an enthusiastic participant in amateur theatre for over twenty years.

Jude won the Society of Women Writers September Writers' Marathon in both 2015 and 2016 and has attained second and third place in two other marathons.

She believes in promoting reading and writing for children and adults alike, at a local level, and is a member of two writers' groups, where she contributes weekly. She is also a member of Sisters in Crime, a group based in Melbourne that provides support for women mystery writers.

Jude loves to travel and experience new things. She wouldn't consider herself an adrenalin junky, but she does like to enjoy life to the fullest. She has parachuted, white-water rafted, ridden a mechanical bull, parasailed, hitch-hiked around Australia, ridden a Harley, and has loved living several times in New York City and New Orleans.